Homage

Homage
Stories

Terence Roberts

Strategic Book Publishing and Rights Co.

Strategic Book Publishing and Rights Co.
USA | Singapore
www.sbpra.com

For information about special discounts for bulk purchases, please contact Strategic Book Publishing and Rights Co. Special Sales, at bookorder@sbpra.net

ISBN: 978-1-62516-954-9

Book Design by Julius Kiskis

22 21 22 20 19 18 17 16 15   1 2 3 4 5

Dedication

In fond memory of Maude Olive Roberts, Audrey Selke, and Canadian artists, David Bolduc and Erik Gamble.

"Shall we ever live? Will we never enter into the picture my mind has painted, this picture which resembles you?"

-Charles Baudelaire
'The Invitation to the Voyage' 1857 - 62

"Art has no task to fulfill in the social, moral, or intellectual context. The artist in society merely has the task of keeping a sense of humanity alive."

-Lucio Fontana

Contents

Homage 1

Oopsy-Poopsy, Again 30

Last Date 38

Colored Spaghetti..52

Meeting Maba 67

Amante Caraqueno...94

Rerun..106

Freeway..135

The Ice Cream Churn..142

Invisible Writing 146

HOMAGE

She was walking beside me, spinning her little silk multi-coloured Japanese purse by its bright red string strap, and I imagined she must have felt happy because I felt happy. It wasn't just because she had popped open the cherry stud buttons of my flannel-checked cowboy shirt the night before, when I had brought her home after seeing a rerun of Leo McCarey's The Awful Truth with Irene Dunne and Cary Grant, and she had promptly summoned me up to her bed. It was also because my bank account was loaded from the award I had just received for contemporary painting.

And of course this was the Elm Street pave with its quiet little side streets left over from Toronto's verdant and cosy infancy, when nothing but tree branches towered over little attic rooms. And isn't it funny how a minor thing like a dip in the pave as it reached the curb facing busy University Avenue could make me feel a little happier? This even though on my left, on both sides of the huge avenue, two sprawling hospitals diffused their faint scent of medicine into the air, and in front of a wing for drug addicts across the street, parallel to the pave, a few junkies rested their drooping heads on their knees, a relative or friend beside them probably whispering words of comfort.

Glancing up at the bronze statue of a Canadian soldier at ease on his pedestal of citations above the narrow promenade between the two-lane avenue, reminded me of the italicized memory inserts in Hemingway's The Snows of Kilimanjaro, which I had always loved. If I were ever going to write, I would be inspired by that. Hemingway had come to mean even more to me when I found out he had worked as a reporter for The Toronto Star, and had lived in this city. But I probably wasn't even thinking any of this as I walked beside Anita along the scantily-used wider Elm Street pave up to Bay Street, where, intending to stroll west to an art gallery, we would catch a bus on the other side to take us uptown to Yorkville.

Bay had changed quite a bit since the 70s, but you could always depend on the Macdonald Block on the southwest corner of Wellesley at Bay to remain visually faithful to the past. There I had recently seen—would you believe it—The Queen's Collection of recent contemporary Canadian painting, which had left me giggling and surprised; I had never associated such zany, quirky exuberant abstract works by painters I knew, with Her Majesty's taste.

At a diagonal from the building, on the northeast corner of Bay and Wellesley was another unchanging monolith—a hotel of suites for resident and visiting celebrities, where, as the bus groaned by on a slight uphill climb, I remembered attending a function at a renowned medical scientist's residence, having been dragged there by my ex-wife. She was probably still in her edgy rebellious stage, knowing damn well she could depend on me to blurt out something startlingly contrary to the whole subdued academic atmosphere, where the only interesting features that night had been an original little Chagall canvas from his blue period, plus the hors d'oeuvres and wine.

And I did embarrass her eventually, if just to confirm my self-conscious awareness that I was the only misfit, beatnik, bohemian, or whatever I thought they thought of me. I remember saying that I thought man hadn't really progressed anywhere, at least not as a human concept, but was still a primitive caveman, an often brutal and insensitive beast. A young German scientist present had been outraged, obviously, since his whole professional faith had been called into question.

By this time I was on the Bay bus with freckle-faced redheaded Anita beside me, and she was chattering away in her haughty dismissive manner about the Nouveau Riche developers who were tearing down all the cosy old walk-up apartment buildings we both loved, replacing them with towering glass castles that remained half occupied because of the rents, but probably with equity enough because of some other viable business option about which we knew nothing. And two corners up from Wellesley, I even forgot to glance up Irwin Street where brownstone suites had recently replaced a particular old walk-up—a walk-up where a year ago I had found myself sleeping every week in my photographer's top-floor apartment.

Anita didn't have a clue about this, since by then I had already fortified my chance affair with her by relishing the similarity of her features and figure to Silvana Mangano's, one of my favourite actresses. Anita's slouched pronounced walk called up other addictive imagistic comparisons with Delphine Seyrig in Last Year at Marienbad as she got off the bus before me in her glove-tight black velvet pants with a thin gold line in relief on the side of each leg, while her small hands—rough from grating cheese and carrots, rolling out dough and baking, washing dishes and scrubbing kitchen counters—fumbled her Capstan Players Light and a box of all-purpose red-tipped matches from the pocket of her pin-striped sports jacket, popped a Capstan to the side of her pink lips, and struck a match on a lamp post.

I saw myself now on the top floor, the fourth, of Stephan's apartment building, walking nervously around in my underwear with a steaming cup of Stephan's special blend of Egyptian coffee, black with honey, and then sitting beneath the white archway in the two-roomed salon. Stephan wasn't around at ten on a bright spring morning; he would have been out with his camera roaming the streets for scenes, having never gotten over David Hemmings' role in Antonioni's Blow Up, the illustrated film script of which was somewhere among dozens of other similar texts, stacks of LPs, art magazines, The New York Times Book Review, The Village Voice, Newsweek, Playboy and Penthouse (nothing much Canadian though, except The Globe and Mail newspaper and a few issues of Saturday Night). All of these surrounded us at hands' reach when we sat on cushions, or when I stretched out on the carpet and fell asleep on one of those nights I didn't return to my big and lonely warehouse studio close to the lakeshore, where the wind seeped through the crevices of the grimy sash windows.

It was Stephan's company I kept, and vice versa, now that it was over between my wife and me. And so our conversations would roll on about Antonioni's scenes and meanings, Stephan's favourite topic, although sometimes the topic would drift to Faulkner and Hemingway, Eldridge Cleaver and Leroi Jones, Miles Davis and Coltrane, Wayne Shorter and Eric Dolphy, Monk and Ron Carter.

The sounds of jazz floating around the bare, faded turquoise apartment walls where during the day sunlight from the one wide western sash window flowed across the salon, hitting the walls of Stephan's little bedroom and the floor stacked with more books, more periodicals, more papers, its aqua-marine core glowing peacefully like a monk's cell. At night the salon's open window allowed us a view of Bay Street with its glittering traffic; it overlooked the priests' quarters on St Michael's College campus and the trees of Queen's Park with more twinkling lights on a roundabout, and invited the closer roar of Yonge Street with its throngs of restless feet and the club music like one huge confused but subdued voice.

Why didn't I ever tell Anita about my time at Stephan's place? Probably because I was so hell-bent on being happy right then with her. And now I was seeing myself at Stephan's place walking on air, barefoot, in my underwear, euphoric in a sado-masochistic way—not just from the psychedelic blotting paper with the green frog printed on it that I had dissolved on my tongue as a form of self-therapy, but from the whole unbelievable personal crisis I had fallen into after seven years of luxury, so to speak.

The crisis—not the luxury—came compliments of my ex-wife who, for most of those years had been thrilled to be by my side on Saturday morning gallery openings in Yorkville, surrounded by the works of Dubuffet, Rauschenberg, Botero or Matta, sipping wine, nibbling hors d'oeuvres, tanned, dressed suavely in chic safari-styled jackets and white slacks like our artist friends in Mexico City and Caracas. My name, our ticket to acceptance, regularly appeared on periodical covers, and our phone rang off the hook each week with dinner invitations to other couples' apartments—couples who sooner or later ended up like us, recounting their different versions of disillusionment when met alone, or strolling with some new "friend" on the same downtown circuit defined by the sidewalks of Bloor and Bay, Charles and Balmuto, Prince Arthur and Bedford.

This divine comedy of mine was probably surmised by Blaise, the cynical Jamaican dandy with a low mulatto hairstyle like an antique bust of Plato or Caesar, who turned up at any hour, day or night, at Stephan's door. His ticket to entry was his well-known love, shared by Stephan, of Baudelaire and Rimbaud, Gore Vidal and Tennessee Williams. He considered the Public Library his office, while living off a dwindling island inheritance, or unemployment insurance, or welfare, in a room no one ever saw. Sometimes he waxed ecstatic about some new solvent woman in his life, but generally he was resolutely resigned to somnambulating through what he described as the pitiful spectacle of human society, which he regarded with simmering scorn.

One night, with a wistful twisted smile like a villainous Richard Widmark in one of his westerns or film noirs, Blaise sat on Stephan's salon floor and said to me, "How the hell did you let a woman do that to you?" To which I had no reply, only a chagrined grin, not just because of the psychedelic altitude of my blood, but because I was enjoying being the subject of attractive negation, the pampered baby lovingly cheered up before being put to bed by Stephan and his friends.

Stephan, with his Douglas Fairbanks looks, often hurried up four flights to our penthouse retreat, bearing a large warm pizza with everything, or boxes of Chinese food and side orders of fried squid, a bottle of Saki or a jumbo Lambrusco, the spoils of some recent photographic assignment. He would fuss around in his little kitchenette's cupboards for plates and wine glasses, sharing them out on the floor, then adjusting the Panasonic mood for my benefit with Bob Marley's "Misty Morning," or Mick Jagger's "Miss You," or Eddie Money's "Two Tickets To Paradise" and "Baby Hold On To Me," all the while casually reminding everyone in the room that nothing really serious had happened to me—only life.

He recounted episodes of his own cuckoldom with women whom he said later ended up as promiscuous hags; then, at our sadistic urgings, he reluctantly retold for the umpteenth time the regrettable night he went out to Yonge Street, picked up a gorgeous redhead at a bar, and returned with her to this very apartment—only to find out she was a man in drag. When he refused to satisfy her, he was given a sound thrashing as a result, relieved of his money, and left with a black eye.

But Stephan's place did have its up side, due to some of his more auspicious conquests, one of which he was kind enough to share with me. One afternoon, when I happened to have the apartment to myself and my depression, I was sober, dressed with nowhere to go, the surrounding downtown familiarity of bookstores, restaurants, boutiques, cinemas, clubs which I once frequented with my wife serving only as a nagging reminder of her absence. On this summer afternoon, I heard a knock at Stephan's door and resisted the urge not to answer. I reasoned that Stephan liked having take-out food delivered before he returned from somewhere, even in the neighbourhood, and by now he knew my habits well enough to be sure I would be in.

It was food all right, the type we both liked. I couldn't believe my eyes. She looked like early Cher, only shorter and browner, with the same long glossy black hair past her shoulders. She wore a fitted white shirt, its open top buttons revealing what were surely avocado-shaped breasts. Her tight shorts were of dark denim with a gold embroidered pocket lining, and her legs were good and slender and deeply tanned, going well with her hand-crafted leather sandals. She seemed a little amused to find me instead of Stephan. For some reason I took this as an uncanny ability to see the mental state I was in, an insight which involved paranoia on my part, so I was already shutting the door in her face when she softly demanded my name. Of course that reminded me I needed hers to inform Stephan that she had been here.

That's when she said, "Luz." But the word didn't register at once, because even my Spanish vocabulary had been stunted by my mental state. After a pause, she added, "As in loose woman."

That I understood instantly. Normally this revelation would have accelerated my customary interest, but instead I found myself blurting out an unnecessary stream-of-consciousness apologetic confession of my present state: my separation, inertia, and depression.

She cut me short by inviting me out for a drink and a walk in the beautiful summer weather. I accepted so unenthusiastically that while locking the door, I suspected she thought I was playing one of those sympathy-catching games of seduction. She took me to a nearby restaurant at the corner of Bay and St Joseph, and we sat under an outdoor café umbrella. She ordered two rounds of the chilled white house wine. As we sipped, she told me she was from Peru—in fact, she had just returned from a visit there—and she designed jewellery, which made me suddenly notice the broad silver baroque band on her right wrist and the coloured stone necklace around her smooth tanned neck.

We discussed Pre-Columbian artefacts and modern Latin American painters like Reveron, de Syzslo, Obregon, Matta, Tamayo, and Botero. We spoke of my time in Caracas and Mexico City, of novels like Cortazar's Hopscotch, Carpentier's The Lost Steps, the poems of Octavio Paz and Gabriel Mistral, and so on. Even as we strolled down St Joseph to Queen's Park, the stares and whistles of young men as we sat on the green grass of the park in sunlight, made me think of that Eric Burden song "Spill The Wine," which I still loved intensely. All this brought home to me my fortunate circumstances in having her at my side—yet I could go no further, her beauty and intelligence already having absorbed both my desire and fear of intimate contact. We didn't return to Stephan's place together. She caught a bus going south down Bay, calling out "Ciao luego!" as she boarded. I went home alone.

When I told Stephan of her visit, all he said was, "Oh yeah, Luz and the Rites of Spring." A year later, I took Anita to an Italian restaurant and found Luz was a part-time waitress there. She seemed happy to see me, in contrast to Anita, who did not seem at all happy to see another woman who treated me with such easy familiarity. This is probably why I never mentioned

Stephan's place to Anita as the Bay bus groaned by Irwin Street on its way to Yorkville Avenue. I had learned that for people like Anita and me, so many streets in this city wore our secrets on their sleeves.

Anita and I were in our thirties now, having kicked around Yorkville without knowledge of each other since our late teens, when the "head scene" was in full swing. We went by what used to be the Crazy David poster shop, and neither of us spoke of the days when we were part of the blissful crowd on one of the side streets, or even right there up ahead on Yorkville Avenue. In those days a black iron fence with a slanted stone rampart to the sidewalk was lined with our standing or sitting bodies, our bright-sashed hats, slim corduroys, vests over silk Moroccan shirts, Beatle boots, sandals or native moccasins, long peasant dresses and blouses, our embroidered denims, as we drifted up the street to Crazy David which would waft us inside with its exotic incense, its pulsating music, its psychedelic Hendrix, Cream, Jefferson Airplane, Santana and Jethro Tull posters. In the darkness everything seemed to undulate, expand and contract before we came back outside, blinking. But I wasn't seeing any of that now, and the address had become a boutique selling crockery and brass.

A little further up the avenue, I noticed an Italian restaurant and outdoor café where Yorkville's best black dance club once stood. I had nothing to say about that either as we went by the once crowded walk-up to the club door, which stood above a few steps going down to a crazily-lit cellar space where young black Americans and Canadians—mostly musicians, pimps, gigolos, and girls who travelled or worked with them—fashionable, slick, and extremely gregarious, lined the front of the club, moving to the beat of bands like the 5th Dimension, Sly and the Family Stone, Martha Reeves and the Vandellas, and James Brown.

I was one of the select few blacks from the West Indies or the Caribbean who went there, though the Americans and Canadians couldn't really tell where I was from, not only because of the way I spoke (I had totally shifted to the standard English tone once reserved for intellectual dialogues back home), but because I never professed an interest in anything other than what we were doing there: hanging out, dancing, sweet-talking, joking, smoking, or drinking inside the club. Since disembarking at Toronto's airport in 1968, I had learnt that an inevitable stereotype derived from an old tropical colonial backwater awaited any revelation of my national origin—which meant there would be no escaping my inferiority to almost everything or everyone indigenous to Canada. The solution was to keep one's origin hidden (as some I knew did), or at least unnoticed.

In my case that was not difficult or even deliberate, since I had never assumed a general national culture anyway; though I grew up with one and knew its folklore, its songs, calypsos, jump-up music, its steel bands, its cricket mania, its often exaggeratingly self-conscious novels, poems, paintings, sculptures, and drama. All this had simply been just a part of countless other cultural interests, like classic Hollywood movies (to me, even more relevant to the still-unexplored historical and social realities of our society), continental European films, classical music, mainstream, swing, and avant-garde jazz, international literature, or pop and soul—all of which I had already absorbed as my culture. In other words, I had no indigenous culture except the one I fashioned for myself as time went by.

It must have been the mute conviviality of such an identity that the tall well-dressed blacks with their stiff broad hats at a slant, who walked or strutted at a slant, their fisted right hands rigid as boards beside their thighs, sensed in my persistent amiable presence outside the club. And one, perhaps secretly encouraged by his girlfriend who swung her hips against mine, wobbled down to the ground and up again, and claimed this was part of a new dance sound called "Disco," once side-stepped up to me and announced, "Hey blood, listen up! You're the kind of cat I need to help me run this stable of bitches I keep in Georgia. Get your things together, man, and let's fly out tonight. How 'bout it?"

And of course he was sort of surprised when I remained unexcited and said, "That's cool, man, but I'm sort of tied up otherwise, you know." Meaning, I was actually enjoying watching, absorbing, and thinking about the experience unfolding around me.

Anita was saying something derogatory about Luigi's, where I said I wanted to take her to an afternoon lunch after we had finished with the galleries. "Luigi's!" she was saying, in that tone that expressed surprise at having anything to do with such a suspect subject; but her eyes and half-smile as she glanced at me hinted at a different surprise, one that felt self-conscious at being treated so romantically. I didn't have to think much to realise I had no realistic estimation of the women I had been dating since my separation. But the boutique with the big bay window we were passing could never erase the fact that it had been my gallery as recently as six months ago, when after moving out of Stephan's place I had found a room in a boarding house off Queen Street, run by a reclusive organic food- obsessed Germanic homosexual and an Afro-Latin busybody music lover.

I had been offered a show by a young gallery owner who had come to Toronto from the Canadian West. As he had not yet been snobbishly jaded by the art world, he had taken someone's recommendation of me, rung me up in the studio and made an appointment to come over. He had liked the generous-sized works on paper stapled to the wall and the whole concept of the discovery and acquaintance of the Americas by nomadic tribes that served as my inspiration at the time. Perhaps he, being acquainted with such a culture as a Westerner, had seen in them the bark and skins, the bones and stones, the seeds and feathers, the water and sky and earth and fire, the cycle of seasons; and maybe he too liked Turok, Son of Stone comics, though we never spoke of it, leaving everything unspoken, but felt and shared.

The Yorkville sidewalk wasn't even one-tenth as crowded now as it was on the night I walked out of my exhibition, half-drunk on wine and very alone. Even though I was thrilled to see the avenue traffic-jammed, the sidewalk packed with people and the café tables so full that I had to move at a snail's pace, I felt a numbing depression that increased with every step I took towards the Yorkville subway's back entrance on Cumberland. It wasn't so hard to remember now how the whole thing had developed that night of the packed and wild opening, the night that had them staring and re-staring at the paintings. That part was interesting to remember now that I was more sober in many ways, but it was no use attempting to pretend that Gina and Liv were the reason I had left my own show that night alone and guilty, and deserving it.

I had told Gina to come early to the exhibition since she had already seen most of the pictures from frequenting my studio and the small room I had rented on shady Sullivan Street off Queen. I had added that I was going to be busy dealing with potential clients as the night wore on, and she shouldn't waste the rest of her night on my account. My real motive was to leave with Liv whom I had told to arrive late, when the opening would be winding down to a close, so we could get away together. How was I to know that Gina would arrive late enough to find Liv already at my elbow every way I turned?

Liv, whom I had only met a month or so after meeting Gina,

seemed to have a completely different approach to seduction that involved New Wave dancing and a captivating form of day-time idling I shared: lying across the big bed of an art student girlfriend of mine at her downtown apartment on John Street a few doors from Queen, where the whole scene between University Avenue and Bathurst Street was at our doorstep. I was immediately fascinated by Liv with her spiky blond hairstyle, her simmering sexual languor I could see rising each time we met, even as she nibbled at her fish and chips and yogurt while turning the pages of the Only Paper Today, Fashion Period, Art Forum or Artscribe. It's always some girlfriend you never lay who either gets you into trouble with one of her girlfriends, or out of trouble with one of your girlfriends.

I had met Gina before I met Liv, at the studio of a girlfriend of hers on the floor below mine in an old ex-warehouse we shared at Berkeley and the Esplanade. Gina's head of thick long black curls, like something out of some of those Florentine or Venetian paintings which represented her Italian heritage, captivated me just like the initial introduction to the haughty flash of her dark eyes in her pale angelic face. She seemed to make estimations and decisions about people—or maybe just about men—in a blindingly short space of time, and whatever she had been told about me (and she had been told a lot, I knew) seemed to demand an adventure of proof.

So her bold assertiveness on our first meeting ended with her phone number at home and work in my possession. The whole thing occurred as though it were obvious I wanted it to happen, even though I hadn't said so. Or let's put it another way: it seemed she was confirming what I wanted but couldn't admit. Maybe it was the way she saw me looking at her hair, or perhaps it was the fact that I spoke so passionately about Fra Angelico, Sonia Delaunay and Viera da Silva, without seeming to realise that such topics, which both girls held their own on, were not half as alive or pleasurable as the flesh-and-blood subject before me. Unquestionably, Gina was determined to reveal the flesh-and-blood desire behind the mask of intellectual shop we were talking.

Whatever reasons motivated Gina, she gave me an invitation to call her at work. I did, one Friday morning a week or so later, when I felt a lull after a hectic week of painting, or confident from the romantic pleasure of surviving on the frugal sale of work to a curator, a motherly sexy publisher of children's books, a young female art dealer, and a rich immigrant accountant from Montreal who had been a neighbour of mine in our home country.

Gina invited me to pick her up after work at the huge studio factory on Queen Street West, where her art college degree enabled her to design art objects and repair stained glass antiques. I had left my rooming house on Sullivan Street, walked south on Beverly and caught a Queen Street tram a block away. Gina rode her bike, so we decided that instead of walking the ten blocks or so back to my place, I would again catch a tram car while she rode parallel to it, and whoever arrived first at Beverly or Soho would wait there. I remember her deep maroon slacks accenting her ample figure as she rode, her light khaki safari jacket held down by the canvas strap of the glossy brown tote bag slung across her back and between the obviously bare breasts beneath her turquoise jumper.

With my elbow on the open window sill of the sliding tram, I felt a thrill seeing Gina's bare feet in blue sneakers rotating below her wild curls swept back by the late spring breeze. We smiled up and down at each other as stores and banks went by before we crossed Yonge Street and my tram made a stop. Gina rode on. Then my tram sped beneath the high walkway connecting the big department stores of Simpsons and Eaton's; after the Law Courts and City Hall, we were over University Avenue and past the old pioneer Heritage House and the Queen Mother Restaurant, before my tram caught up with Gina who had stopped outside Dragon Lady Comics, one of my favourite stores.

She was balanced on her saddle, the tips of her sneakers just touching the asphalt, her hands folded across her chest as she shared a joke with a good-looking blonde girl in a light shiny silver raincoat with a fuchsia tote bag slung across it. She had one hand on Gina's bike handle, gesticulating with the other, giggling as she tossed her head of bouncy styled hair.

I ended up at Soho's corner before Gina, and as we went by the Black Bull tavern where "Echo Beach" by Martha and the Muffins was playing, she poked a finger through the rent in the right elbow of my black leather bomber jacket, the kind with little zips on the sleeves, which a rocker friend had bequeathed me. She hooked her left hand through my right in the pocket of my cream slacks, and she wheeled her bike with her free hand as we walked down Soho, turned left at Phoebe, then right at Huron, then right again on Sullivan, and arrived home.

We left her bike on the ground floor hallway and sat in the kitchen at a plain rustic old oak table before a chilled bottle of Turinese dry white Gavi some friends had recently given me as a gift on their return from Italy. I brought out my precious slab of perforated dry Argentine cheese, which titillated Gina's taste buds. Her body heat probably leaped even higher when I quickly cooked shredded smoked herring with tomatoes, onions, garlic and hot tropical peppers, which we ate with brown rice. Gina, as I think I said before, was not the timid type, so it was she who suggested we go upstairs to my room to smoke a joint that her Queen Street girlfriend had given her—or rather us, Gina added, sending one of her meaningful looks my way.

It was a small room, with a one-window view to the wild backyard. It contained a well-prepared mattress on the floor, a clothes cupboard, a table and chair. But what interested Gina were the three free-hand structured watercolours influenced by the prehistoric Americas, which she studied in silence from the edge of the mattress where we sat with the smoking joint wrapped in thin perfumed cherry-flavoured paper passing between us. Abruptly Gina opened her tote bag and brought out a bottle of Amaretto liqueur, giving it to me to open, and I remember I wanted to make her gift the opportunity to at least begin to kiss her on the cheek or neck.

But before I could move, she asked if I had milk and glasses, and I said yes, and she ran out the door and down the stairs barefoot to get them. For the first time, I found myself staring at the lettering on the Amaretto bottle as though I had never seen them before, as though it had suddenly become a treasure. And after I read the fine print on the back label which said it was an ancient blend created by an Italian lady for an artist who was her lover, I knew I would have to make love to Gina with all the finesse I could muster that night.

I recall now the ecstatic sound of her voice as we made love (without any protection on my part, since there were no herpes or AIDS at that time). I remember she asked me to stop after it was apparent we'd had simultaneous orgasms, yet I remained hard and mobile. The fact that she snored and left no room for me on the small bed, and the enormous circular stain she left and I slept on for weeks, became all part of my affection for her. We began a loose uncommitted affair, with no demands, instead with sudden and exciting dates resulting from requests from either one of us—like when I took her to a Third World concert at Massey Hall, and afterwards outside, endured the tight-lipped accusing eyes of friends who had socialised closely with my wife and I before our separation; or when she called me up one night when I was engrossed in some discussion with other artists, yet

I left them to meet her at the Maple Leaf Gardens to hear Joan Armatrading. What remains with me from that night is not the music, which was more her interest, but the two unforgettable times when, thirsty from the heat of bodies and smoke, she went off through the crowd and brought back paper cups of ice water. I can still see her walking calmly back to me down the aisle with the cups before her, an enigmatic serenity on her face.

There had to be a downside to our very considerate and tolerant affair. That came one night when I took her to see Lina Wertmuller's Swept Away at the Medical Arts Building film program on the U of T campus. I of course had seen it before, but Gina hadn't, and yet I don't recall wanting her to see it out of any identification with Giancarlo Gianini's role as the working class sailor who ended up marooned on a deserted island with the rich spoilt wife of an industrialist, acting out the dominant class structure roles in reverse, as his masculine survival skills and love-making prowess tamed her to domestic subservience. Who among the departing audience would have thought that this apparently homogeneous couple—Gina resplendent in her Hookers Green velvet coat, her black curls shiny and bouncy, the thin red belt in her black slacks like a rush of exposed electricity around her slender waist, and I my usual dapper self—would end up almost at the end of our affair over the implications of a movie?

And yet in retrospect I realise how deeply I had doubted both my own and her achievements, and how paranoid I had been at the time, unable to fathom why a few students should rush ahead of us as we descended the long staircase, opening doors, allowing us to pass through like celebrities. The fact that I had written a number of serious essays on art in the city's popular avant-garde journals had been self-dismissed to unread oblivion, just as Gina's public works of art seemed to exist in my imagination alone.

But from the moment we reached the campus sidewalk, and all the way down McCaul, across Grange Park into John Street (where I remember seeing light in the art student's apartment where I had first met Liv), onto Queen and to the Black Bull tavern, our arguments raged for and against the implications of that unforgettable film. I still don't know if Gina was provoking that non-romantic side of me that she must have noticed in other discussions, but perhaps accelerated by two or three glasses each of draft from the large jug before us, the argument continued, maybe even in subconscious imitation of scenes in the Wertmuller film we had just seen.

Suddenly, abruptly, I came to my limit, called for the bill, and said I thought it was best our relationship come to an end then and there. I remember Gina calmly stretching forward, placing her beautiful hand on mine on the table and quietly saying she didn't want that at all, not at all. After which, we drank a bit more, changed the subject, and spoke with various people we knew who were entering or leaving the tavern; then, at her urging, we caught a street car over to her house, picked up half a dozen eggrolls at a nearby late night Chinese delicatessen on the way, and made love fiercely three times. (The last time was only possible due to her expertise in muscle movement above me.)

In the morning, looking quite domestic or even childish in her nightgown, she went through one of those scenes where girls show their boyfriends various items of memorabilia and nostalgic collections they cherish. Some of hers, pulled from somewhere beneath her bed, were the colour photo cut-outs of a safari where a lioness chased and devoured a monkey, in serial shots. I had the uncanny feeling that we were each related to those animals. She was bound in totemic relationship to the lioness, as I was to the monkey. I suspected that our argument had not really ended, only taken a detour.

It could have been the smouldering embers of that argument that had pulled me deeper into Liv's circle at her girlfriend's apartment. That, and the fact that something infectiously colourful, musical and socially wild had sandwiched me between Gina and Liv. "Love," as the song said, "was in the air." There seemed to be something atmospheric and altruistic out in the streets and neighbourhoods, the studios, cafés, bookstores, art galleries, and nightclubs we frequented on Queen, King, Front, Spadina, Adelaide, Richmond, and all their cross-street tributaries.

Being with Liv and her friends now seemed to come in crackling bright cellophane in a kaleidoscope of colours, especially when we strolled down to the Queen Mother, Beggar's Banquet, the Parrot, or the Horseshoe. I loved it when Liv—her face set in serene serious precision—couldn't help undulating to the opening bars of Blondie's "Rapture," or when we each floated in the current of the Police doing "Walkin' on the Moon" and "Don't Stand So Close to Me," or the English Beat's "Mirror in the Bathroom," or the Cars doing "She Likes the Nightlife." These waves of sound swept us in or delayed us outside the big glass fronts of Queen Street's night spots.

Those events now seemed a daze in which I recognised only the ghost of my present self, a dancing ghost who each week had shed or tried to shed the skin but not the shadowy spirit of my marital memories along with the plunge into uncertainty my career as an artist suffered. My emotional state was played out on some dance floor among many strangers, many of whom reached out in friendship from some dark chamber of experiences similar to mine, but which we had neither the time nor the inclination to discuss.

Liv was a soothing, intimate possibility of anonymous corporeal company, while Gina became merely a strange voice on the line, distant but friendly, like a favourite masochistic wound that was still healing. My clairvoyant mind imagined radii of longing silently transmitted to me from Gina's remote location on some desert island, and then I was suddenly brought back to reality by her voice calmly explaining that she was busy with friends from a rural commune who were visiting for a few weeks at her place. Once I must have provoked one of her frank responses with some enquiry which was settled by her casual reply; "Yes, there is sex."

Liv's voice, on the other hand, enthusiastically told me of native drums she heard at night near her hometown in Saskatchewan, and how she and her little brothers had danced pow-wow to the sound. Liv became an easy preference over Gina. The next thing I knew I was picking Liv up one night at her uptown apartment on Bedford Street, small but affordable on her salary as an interior design consultant. By then we had agreed we loved to dance, so it was not unusual that Liv said I looked like Kool in my off-white Spanish canvas shoes, matching pleated front cuffed slacks, and shirt open down to the sternum over a tight red t-shirt.

We walked all the way down Yonge Street, past clubs infectiously booming Kool and the Gang's "Too Hot" and "Ladies' Night," Gino Vanelli's "I Just Want to Stop" and "People Gotta Move." Liv sparkled in navy blue spandex trousers, with a sleeveless black and white striped T-shirt, her spiky blonde hair-style turning vermilion, turquoise, orange or blue in the overhead neon. Our shoulders twisted through the throng as her Chloe fragrance came and went, raising my senses, and sometimes I heard the shrill call of my name by people I barely knew or recognised, the sound and the caller quickly lost in the thick flow of the sidewalk's river.

One night we went to a New Wave basement club on one of those backstreets off the curving tram car tracks near Yonge and

Dundas. It turned out I knew the young mulatto doorman who was the drummer for an up-and-coming pop band, and he let us in free. There were others I knew in the club, but I made sure I was the only one who bought drinks for Liv, though Liv was not the only one who bought drinks for me. She was mostly on the packed floor alone, with everyone's partners coming and going, intermingling like the kinetic spot-lights that bathed everyone in multi-colours as they bounced from side to side. They shadow-danced on their rubber-soled canvas shoes to the paradisiac, ecstatic spatial rhythms of "Planet Earth," "Is There Something I Should Know?," "Message in a Bottle," "Cruel to be Kind," "Call Me," "High School Confidential," "Echo Beach," "Pina Colada," "Venus," "Don't Stop Till You Get Enough," "The Beat Goes On," and "Could You Be Loved."

The sound bounced off the walls, flowing around and through me as I sipped Kahlua with ice. I watched Liv's drink diluting in her sweating glass as she worked up real sweat on the dance floor, sometimes leaning forward to hear what someone beside her was saying. Liv must have been wondering if I was ever going to join her, but just then I heard that new song that had taken the artists in my circle by surprise, astonishing us by its resonance with the ideas we were concocting out of the structures of so many cultures in our studios: I mean "Moving Down a Straight Line," and Liv recognised that I would want her to myself for this one, the unspoken memory of knowing this song already as obvious to her as it was to me. It was a sudden magical justification for this night we had taken for ourselves.

Later that night she introduced me to someone, a man younger than I was, handsome and white, dressed in tight black jeans and a matching leather jacket. Clearly they were old friends, so I left them to themselves and enjoyed my nest of male friends at the bar beside the short stairway to the club. It was the kind of atmosphere I knew well, in which people lost control of their initial intentions, although not necessarily in a negative way. All the drinks and special cigarettes that appeared out of nowhere served as an inspiration for philandering the night away. This new direction gained control over my night's original agenda, in which Liv and her friend had become mere ingredients dissolved.

That's when I felt her hand on my arm and turned around to see her lingering face, like a blurred mask, no longer flaunting the clarity it wore when we first arrived. She announced that "we" were leaving, while her friend stood by like a confident success. I had interpreted "we" to mean the two of them, and I was already waving her off with a smile and the usual promise of "I'll call you," already turning back to my friends and the drink beside me, only to have her statement further clarified: "You're coming with us." Am I? And she was pulling me off my stool to the laughter of my friends, who began cryptically joking about some "trail horse hitched to its buggy in front."

Outside there was a nice chill from short fountains above a shallow pond. Here I refreshed my face while Liv, who had assumed control of our party to the visible discomfort of her silent beau, kept calling my name ecstatically and expressing a desire to be taken dancing to another club. So I suggested Mama G's, where she had never been, just around the corner on Yonge, with the Hard Rock Café visible at the other corner up ahead. But on the pave outside Mama G's, which was another basement affair with two stairs at right angles going down into a buzzing supernova galaxy out of which Gino Vanelli's "Love of my Life" surfaced like an SOS, the young Italian doorman and bouncer accepted only me, rejecting Liv and her friend, apparently due to their punk/rock attire. Her beau at that point expressed his indignation, snarling that he preferred the Hard Rock Café anyway. But Liv protested that she wanted to dance, and there was no real dancing there. Realizing Liv had unexpectedly been embarrassingly caught in some prior relationship about which I knew nothing, I decided to encourage her to continue the night with her friend, and promised that we'd catch up again.

I remember Liv's eyes with their silent mixture of frustration and apology looking back over her shoulder as she walked away beside the young man toward the Hard Rock Café.

I vanished into Mama G's like a suicidal maniac, a perfect choice for the starring role in the Ray Charles number "Born to Lose" (if that song were ever made into a movie). I intended to stick to the bar, beginning with the strongest drink the remainder of my money could afford. From the bottom of the last little stairs the half-packed club and almost empty dance floor looked like the void, its bar in a corner with male and female loners, and couples and groups at tables.

Facing the club floor, I felt worse when I recognised Gina beside her blonde girlfriend and a suave-looking Italian guy, a conceptual artist-photographer with whom I'd once shared an issue of an art periodical. I realised he was Gina's girlfriend's lover. It would have been impossible for us to avoid speaking, so finally Gina asked what I was drinking. When I said it was a stinger, the smiling artist wagged his head and finger at me, as if to say, "Naughty boy."

The stinger went down cool yet warm in little sips while I noticed Gina discreetly glancing me over. She had on a short green skirt below a striped pink and blue silk shirt that ended at her waist, with no bra, and I had to take a large gulp of my cocktail when I recognised that the fragrance oozing in mysterious bursts from her nape and bosom was Chloe. The whole atmosphere between us was too tense and I took the blame silently, until in a burst of impatience with the syrupy black music that was on, and a desire to access my situation, I whispered in Gina's ear, "So how's everything been?"

She smiled into the highball she was nursing and said, "Okay. How about you?"

I said, "I'm trying."

Suddenly the tempo of the music changed into the upbeat tempo of "I'd Do Anything for You." That got us onto our feet, and before the middle of "Let Nobody Tell You What to Do," the whole floor was packed as people began to pour into the club after midnight. We danced through "Sweet Sensation," "Shame," "Upside Down," and "Good Times," but it was at the end of "I'm Coming Out" that the four of us decided to exit onto the hectic late-night summer pave of Yonge Street, where Gina and I wound up in the same Diamond cab.

As Gina and I sped over to her place, I began to re-acquaint myself with the marble smooth gloss of her almost-touching inner thighs, which before we reached her bed upstairs had opened to their fullest on her living room couch, my hands sliding over and beneath the silk of her shirt, massaging the warmth of her spine and breasts, as she whispered my name, adding, "Light me up, it feels like ages!"

The following morning, after explaining to her wild head of black curls tangled against blue silk pillows that I was going to be busy at my studio during the entire week, putting the finishing touches on my upcoming exhibition in Yorkville, and that I'd call to tell her the details of the opening, I caught an early morning street car on Queen back to Soho Street.

I hadn't forgotten Liv or made up my mind she was just an affair that was never meant to be. She couldn't be judged by the events of one night, I thought. And she said so too, apologetically, the following night on the phone, explaining how she had been determined to run away from an immature affair she started over a year ago in Saskatchewan with the intruder of the night before, who had been a fellow university student back there. He was in Toronto now, she said, pursuing a job in journalism, but liked to pass himself off as a rock musician on weekends when he came to the club scene. She said he wanted a commitment but she didn't, so she had decided to simply phase out their relationship by doing exactly what she liked, which meant seeing me.

I thought this was a bit too complicated, so I said, "Hey, Liv, it was really nice being with you, but maybe things will work out for you and this guy. I don't want to spoil it."

That's when she said, "You're going soft on me, is that it? Now when I need you more than ever!"

Perhaps, I thought, if we knew each other better on the inside, where our bodies began feeling the sensation of each other's flesh, we might turn a corner. So I told her to come to my opening in Yorkville the following Saturday evening. It dawned on me that perhaps the glamour of the event would quickly bring Liv to her knees, and we might feel so satisfied with our new sexual knowledge of each other that we'd lose some of our anxiety.

After Liv came off the line, I called Gina and confirmed the date of my opening. Her voice was soft and low as if still in the after-glow of our love-making. She jokingly asked if I'd get her pizza after the show.

"Aren't you the one who should do that?" I asked, teasing her back.

She said she could make homemade pizza if I wanted some, and I said I would take her up on that on Sunday, the day after my opening. I invited her to drop by the opening early in the evening, since she knew most of the works already. I suggested she should go home early for a good night's rest, because the following night I would be keeping her up.

But how was I to know Liv and Gina would ignore my orders

and both turn up early? I introduced Stephan to Gina, hoping he would melt the ice I could see turning the gallery into an igloo. But when I overheard him trying to capitalize on her name by comparing her to Gina Lollobrigida, and her repeated cold reaction of "Oh really," I knew she would not give an inch and allow Liv to get the better of me.

So there we were, the three of us lost for words, standing in a half-circle as though aware that some horrible mute clandestine compact had been made between us, yet none of us could pinpoint it. That's when Liv with a cold precise seriousness of tone I had forgotten she had, abruptly asked Gina, "Aren't you here to see the paintings? Then why are you still standing here?"

Gina, with that haughty reserve she could switch on and off in a second, neither replied to Liv or looked at her; she looked at me, her eyes wide and her angelic face a little flushed, like a film beaming the hidden events of our last intimate night together with a tacit emotional accusation.

I melted into the guests at my show. Maybe I went over to a painting and pretended to straighten it on its strings—I think I did—then vanished into the throng of other friends, guests and clients. I never saw when Gina or Liv left. They never notified me. Maybe they left together? I neither phoned them nor did they phone me. I neither visited their apartments, or their friends' apartments, or saw them on the street, or in stores, or anywhere, except perhaps in fleeting mobility.

Anita and I had arrived at our destination and were walking up the short stairs to an art gallery almost at the end of Yorkville, a few doors before the traffic lights at busy Avenue Road. Anita was asking, now that we were almost there, what was so compelling about this gallery show we were about to see. It was just like her to ask such a naive question when the answer could already be seen on the walls as we opened the glass door and confronted the first of maybe a dozen Jean-Paul Riopelle abstract canvasses in various dimensions. Art for Anita had remained Da Vinci, Titian, Munch, Klimt, and Beardsley, whose works could be seen on dust-caked postcards stuck around the creases of the vanity mirror in her bedroom, and she may have been overwhelmed by the difference in the art she knew and the art she now saw mounted before her. Anita brought up the household name of the Canadian Group of Seven, the most famous group of national painters of the local landscape, along with Emily Carr—not, I knew, as a reference to any similarity, or even obvious continuity she had perceived between Riopelle's abstract canvasses and theirs, but as a form of resistance to what she felt she was being asked by me to accept.

Mention of the Group of Seven now catapulted me back to the history of the gallery we had passed a few minutes ago where I had exhibited on that dreadful night of Gina and Liv's collision. During its later existence, its owner, the young Westerner, had been approached with an offer to purchase one of the Group of Seven works at its standard enormous price, which was exactly the total savings of the gallery owner, who knew he could re-sell the canvas at a good profit out West in a couple of years. It turned out the famous work he bought was an expert fake. He lost the savings that could have ensured that his gallery would still have been there, instead of the boutique we had just passed. And like my episodes with Gina and Liv, that was the end of that.

In the second room, where the hallway led to the gallery's administrative offices and left the longest wall for the display of Riopelle's largest canvas, a good ten feet by five, we stood staring into the vortex of a galaxy made by Riopelle's trowel, loaded with colours picked up simultaneously and pulled across the canvas no more than four or five inches at a time, until the whole canvas had become an opaque yet transparent space.

"Like butterscotch ripple ice cream," Anita said.

"Like milk chocolate bars," I said.

"Like Quality Street bonbons and their wrappers," she said.

"Like Black Forest cake with walnut and mixed-fruit filling," I said.

"Like a roast beef sandwich with mayonnaise, ketchup, and mustard," she said.

By then our bodies were touching, and our hands finding each other's hips, bellies, necks. Influenced by all those references to edibles we had invented from the staggering display before us, our mouths found each other and for minutes remained stuck together. Anita's tongue thrust into my ear like a male organ, reversing our coital roles, a vision that she as much as I must have continued to entertain while we dined on raviolis and green pesto sauce sprinkled with Mozzarella cheese at Luigi's, a corner away from the gallery. We drank an entire bottle of chilled white Chianti before anxiously catching a taxi back to her place near Elm, in whose middle room, on her loft bed, I now found myself plunging into a whirlpool as soft and sweet as the contents suggested by the large Riopelle canvas we had contemplated earlier.

My homage to the painter was somehow now inspired by the imaginative ingredients of his canvases that had become realistically intermingled with the constant diet of banana milkshakes loaded with brewer's yeast, effervescent spicy apple cider, yogurt, liverwurst sandwiches and cheddar cheese muffins Anita and I consumed, making my post-coital languor a delicious feeling of levitation, of floating, as I watched her nude Coca-Cola-bottle body walking out the bedroom towards the kitchen down the hall for refreshments. This made me remember half of a large milk-chocolate bar I had left in her freezer. I called to her to take the chocolate bar from the icebox and bring it back to bed, and I heard her voice in the hallway giggling in that baby-like tone of hers, "The chocolate bar! Coming up!"

OOPSY-POOPSY, AGAIN

"If you could read my mind love"
Gordon Lightfoot

Yesterday he was on the line again asking if she wanted to see this new film with one of his favorite acting couples, Marcello Mastroianni and Sophia Loren, over at the Sheraton Center's cinema. Oh well, why not? It was not going to be easy to ignore or forget or even stop doing so many interesting and enjoyable things they had done together before their separation.

She was obviously still interested in him, and in seeing him. His imagination? Well, it was not he alone who went over mentally all the things they had done during their seven years of living together. Her voice certainly sounded upbeat, in that way he knew well, as though she had been waiting for some offer to do something this weekend. But was that offer supposed to be from him, or from anyone? Or had she already had other offers, turned them down, but accepted his? He wasn't going to ask of course.

What was this film going to be about anyway? Probably something that reflected exactly what they were going through right now as a separated couple. He was that sort of intellectual. Always trying to put you on the spot. Showing you some film, giving you some book which reflected the same thing you were experiencing…or he thought you were experiencing, at present. But of course not telling you straight out. Even though this must be some new film he never saw before, he must know something

30

about it? That's why he called and invited her to go with him?

She was trying to break away from his influence, he knew that. He couldn't blame her. During their entire relationship he had been the leader. She still had that ingrained belief in the traditional nuclear family; not that she didn't have opinions of her own, and very different from his, after all why had they ended up like this now? No, she had simply given him the chance to be the 'man', the father-figure when they were together; but his intellectual and artistic powers had not been sufficient on a practical or 'real' level, as her father would say, to support her and their young daughter, or even himself, and he had failed miserably as a husband. That could be the reason she had made such an about turn and started dating a garbage man, but a degree-holding graduate student nevertheless, who worked with his hands in big dirty gloves during the night while neighborhoods snored. Her father would have liked that if he knew.

Actually, she had really enjoyed the last film he had invited her to at the little Backstage cinema on Balmuto St opposite the Manual Life center: Wife-Mistress, with Mastroianni of course, and Laura Antonelli as his wife-mistress, in the sense that he accepts her being shared with other men. It was a bit too embarrassing seeing it with him though…that scene with Mastroianni looking up at the shutters from the sidewalk after seeing Antonelli bring in her beau, knowing she was about to make love to another man up there! And she seated right beside him in the dark watching this!

He was probably trying to tell her how accepting he was of her sexual freedom now. Waiting for her outside the cinema in some wrinkled green trench coat, (he said he had bought at some trendy recycled clothing store called Flying Down To Rio; named after another movie of course) with the collar up and a cigarette at the side of his mouth like he was Dana Andrews in Laura, or world-weary Yves Montand in Live For Life. Both films he had taken her to in their happier years. She had ended up telling Forrest, the garbage man graduate intellectual she met at therapy sessions, (something to do with authoritarian parents was his problem, apparently) …she had ended up telling him about this film Wife -Mistress he had taken her to, and Forrest had laughed and said he couldn't stand Mastroianni's existential indifference! Like in La Dolce Vita, one of the two or three Mastroianni films he had seen, when Lex Barker slaps him after he returns his wife, Anita Eckberg, at the end of their gallivanting in Rome, and Mastroianni takes it like some sensitive playboy. She and the garbage man had laughed their heads off, seeing themselves as more simple and 'real' people. And just for the hell of it, after putting her daughter to bed in her basement bedroom, then watching Klute with Jane Fonda on late night TV (more their kind of film), they had made love 'coitus interuptus' on the living room couch, agreeing that the garbage man would deliberately leave a spurt of semen at the end of a cushion, so that when he had his visiting rights the next evening he would notice it.

That was the kind of experiment she liked, giggling at its conception. But the next evening he had visited, sat right there on the same cushion before the TV, then left without mentioning the stain beside him. But she knew he had seen it, and was sure he was too embarrassed to say anything.

He was sure she was enjoying the new sense of power these films he invited her out to transmitted, though of course she would never admit that to him, or to anyone else, except maybe her girlfriends. It wasn't the kind of thing you admitted to any man, especially one who had been your lover and husband. It was their secret, he surmised, this power she had which seemed to have been eroded by the more mundane reasoning and influence of her family and friends, but which he was stealthily repairing, not with any ulterior motive of getting back together with her, mind you (she had made it perfectly clear she didn't want that), but just for the sake of friendship, and the child of course. And well… yes, sex, damn it!

In their case, their situation now, what was sex if not the memory of it? He was confident about his power there, even though he knew she was trying to erase these memories. She had to, if she was never going to get back with him. Yet, was it possible to erase a quality still attached to other things, other habits? Like a few months ago when he had gone over to her house on visiting rights and discovered a stack of the same jazz recordings he had introduced her to: 'Return To Forever', 'Weather Report', 'Compost', 'The Charles Lloyd Quartet', Gato Barbieri's: 'Flight of the Phoenix', etc. He had taken her to live concerts by these artists, where she had seen the power of women who handled the financial affairs of the musicians. Once she shook Gato's tiny hand in his blue mitts, and saw a band-leader urging his stoned trumpet player to perk up as they walked in. Copies of the very records he had taken with him when they broke up were back in the bookcase, re-bought by her. Did she tell this new garbage man guy she had made passionate and prolonged love to him many times while those records were playing? Was she trying to do over what she had done with him, or rather, relive their passion secretly by a fetishistic relationship to music they had shared? Of course he would never know, and maybe that's what she intended with these tantalizing clues that made him sleuth, and her slut.

She wondered what would transpire between them tonight when they went to this new film? Not that she was thinking or hoping for anything in particular to occur, but at the same time she was not against the possibility of something transpiring. It felt more exciting like this, she had begun to realize, when there was some possibility of pleasure that came without compulsory continuity. She was in the driver's seat, now that they were separated. It was amazing this pleasure of personal secrecy no one else could know, and which turned like a reel of memories projected on a screen only she could see. The best scenes on that screen, she felt, had a lot to do with his spontaneous reactions to her actions, or attire, or just her presence. That, she had remained vulnerable to, even, admittedly, provoking it at times. Like once when the three of them (the little girl in the middle), were sitting on the couch before some program the child liked on TV, on one of those week-nights he was allowed to visit, and she had suddenly stood up and without a word went down to her basement bedroom, leaving them there, knowing that when he didn't see her return after about ten minutes, he would come down. And he did, finding her lying naked on her side on the sheets, exactly like that scene in Eric Rohmer's Chloe In The Afternoon, one of the films he had taken her to, and which she had loved, realizing her close resemblance to the character Chloe, in features, figure, and even many personal mannerisms. So without any talk, just silent exhilaration, she had swung her long legs over the edge of the bed and they had made love swiftly and deliciously, before the child finally discovered what they were up to and plunged between them happily.

Another time, when she had heard on her female grapevine about one of his recent trysts with some young New Wave fashion designer with henna tinted hair, and had instantly grown jealous, she had donned red shorts a bit slack around her upper thighs and sat provocatively around the house with one leg up beside her. This was when he had come on one of his weekly visits. Of course he behaved as if he hadn't been seeing anyone when asked what he had been up to lately, merely mentioning some new structural problem in painting he was working on. But it could have been her appearance and behavior which curbed any frank urge on his part to mention another woman who was keeping his spirits up, since he must have seen a chance to lay her once again before he left that night. And quite suddenly he had stopped beside her chair and slid his right hand along the inside of her thighs, into the space between her shorts and panties, finding that tender spot he wanted, and she had wanted him to find, yet took his hand away, saying: "It's too early."

What did she mean by that? He didn't ask of course. And even if he did she would probably have evaded him with one of those cryptic remarks she had picked up from one of her man-hating recent girlfriends: "What do you think!" When in fact she meant it was too early for him to have her after having another woman. At least that's what he thought. After all she wasn't going to play some tennis match according to his rules!

They agreed he would meet her on the carpeted lobby of the cinema before the ticket booth, at the bottom of the huge winding staircase leading up to an usher. She had left the child with her elder sister who would sleep over, since she had said she had no idea how late she would be out. She drove her small Renault downtown and left it at a parking lot at Richmond and University. He walked down Queen west from his private new studio on Adelaide, which was a progression from the one he had first shared on the cold and windy esplanade of lakeshore, and whose first month's rent she had paid, like a mother helping her son who was venturing out into a 'man's life' after years of being little more than a child masquerading as a gigolo. He was paying her the respect due to a great mistress he had married, since they had decided to have a child after "tying the knot" casually at City Hall without even a ring, but a Chinese jade bracelet, until he, on a trip he had made to South America, had brought back a broad band of finely carved gold, which turned out to be a bit too slack for her fourth finger.

It was like old times in the cinema, and she felt so excited she ran off to get a jumbo tub of popcorn and two Sprites as the coming attractions began. She seemed to have forgotten, he, a serious film buff, was never excited about popcorn and pop, yet silently, pleasantly, joined her without objection.

Oopsy-Poopsy was hilariously delightful: Mastroianni and Loren at their best going through many ins-and-outs of their relationship, before coming back together again at the end. After the lights came up they walked down the aisle slowly, in good spirits, as though reluctant to see their date come to an end, and she suddenly felt as though her relationship with him was no different than anyone of those girls in the arts scene she knew he slept with, probably over in his new studio, (which she had never seen) now that his name as a painter was on the rise. At the top of the staircase before their descent among other couples openly more affectionate to each other than they were, she said quickly, in that confident casual manner she knew he hadn't forgotten: "Take me to your studio."

He knew what that meant, and it caught him totally unprepared. "I can't," he said, feebly, "someone's in there." She stopped on the stairs, turned to him, and against her self-control uttered: "You mean you have a woman living with you already!" "No," he said, "Stephan…you remember Stephan? The photographer, who let me stay over at his place on Irwin whenever I liked, after we separated? Well, his whole building was ordered shut by the Bailiff, the owner hasn't been paying his municipal bills, everyone's things are locked in there until a lawyer sorts out the issue. He has nowhere else to stay, so I took him in until he gets back on his feet again. You know how it is."

She couldn't find any words of reply. They were out on York

St now. "I'll walk you to your car," he said. "No, that's OK," she replied curtly. "C'mon, it's all in my way," he said. They walked to her parking lot in silence. On the Richmond pave she said good night to him and moved quickly to her car. "Yeah, drive carefully," he said, and walked off, slowly crossing University Avenue where traffic was moving at a fairly slow pace.

His watch said 11pm. He walked down an almost deserted Richmond west, heading up to Spadina, in the direction of a park near his studio with the huge poster of a girl in a bikini sucking up her cocktail on a white Caribbean beach against the wall of a building outside his studio window. Wind whipped dust, newspapers, and torn posters advertising Pop bands along the sidewalk before him as he walked, his hands in the pockets of his Brazilian re-cycled green Varig trench coat. There was a slight smile on his face as he remembered Mastroianni in one of his favorite Mastroianni/Loren films, Yesterday, Today, & Tomorrow, walking down a highway with Loren's expensive car stalled behind him. That was after she had hitched a ride with an eager affluent-looking motorist, leaving Mastroianni to find his own ride. Her left on car radio reeling off the rise and fall of the day's stocks and bonds behind his walking back.

LAST DATE

"I walked into such a sad time at the station."
"White Room" *Cream*

They kept running into each-other after being introduced at a studio party. Now here they were again in a coffee shop at the corner of King and John Streets. He had walked over from his ground floor room on McCaul Street, intending to catch a street car east, up to Sherbourne, then continue walking a few blocks south to his studio on the lakeshore esplanade. He decided he would make a play at her since he still felt the same high voltage between them. It was 8.30 in the morning and he wanted to pick up a fresh bagel with cream cheese, a slice of the day's carrot cake, and a piping hot coffee, taking them into his studio where, first thing, he would sit in his low-down easy chair before the canvas he had started to paint the day before.

She was sitting alone at a small round table for two in a corner before the big glass window with a view of the old Victoria theatre across the street, and the entrance to a mall that took you down a steep escalator and through various corridors, past the patio of the Roy Thompson's Music Hall, and to the King St subway. She was nibbling on a buttered croissant and sipping her hot chocolate while reading a Penguin edition of Francoise Sagan's Silken Eyes, a short story collection. He paid, and picked up his bag of snacks, and though he felt she must have noticed his entrance yet said nothing, he interpreted that as a modest invitation because of the mood he was in. "Oh Hi," she said, looking up when she realized the person coming over to her table wasn't really a stranger. He could have referred to her book of short stories, which he had read, but rejected that as too intellectually easy an introduction. "You're up early," he said, adding, "You live around here?" She laughed a bit, "No, I work around here at a fashion designer's studio, just west of Spadina."

"So that's why we keep running into each-other in this area! Do you like it here better than where you live?" He was edging up to where that was.

"You can say that. It's just conveniently cheaper over at the Annex, but I really don't know anyone in that neighborhood," she said.

"The Annex!" he said, "Gosh, I spent some really exciting years there."

"You know Kendall Avenue then?" she said.

"Kendall! I lived there, what? About three times on the same street, twice at the same address! But to be honest, I haven't seen around there for at least half a dozen years." It was a good point, totally impromptu though.

"Well why don't you come on over sometime and refresh your memory?"

"When?" he said, hopping on it, after all the voltage was there.

She sipped her hot chocolate. She had finished her croissant just before he came over. "How about this evening, say around six, if that's ok, I'll find something to eat and drink."

"Done!" he said, smiling, then, "Listen, I gotta run, I've got work waiting."

"Me too," she said laughing, and got up. As they left she gave him her address.

A street car stop was just outside the café, and as the cars were mostly regular at that time of morning he saw the red and white bulk of one crossing Spadina towards him.

Was he really attracted to her, or was he just after the opportunity she offered for seduction? Watching her walk up King's sidewalk in black slacks with a glossy sheen, a tight navy blue shirt that ended at her waist, and light foam-bottomed purplish boots laced up her insteps, sustained a vague desire in him that had something to do with the lazy, languid, and subtly vulgar manner of her short steps which threw her rounded hips and buttocks from side to side, as though they were lacking some essential discipline, or steerage, only male guidance, his, could provide.

Each time he had seen her before, she had never seemed 'recent'. There were always lines beneath her eyes, as though she hadn't had a good night's sleep, or, if she did have a lover, he, or she, hadn't been adequate. Her auburn hair was cut short, combed to one side in that style with a sleek heavy top and shaved nape, as though she hadn't firmly decided about her gender, or, maybe was just looking for a way to avoid all that female fussiness involving constant trips to coiffeurs. Her features were a bit broad and sensual, like one of those market girls selling vegetables, fruit, or fish in 17th century Flemish still lives. He liked that.

Alone, before his unfinished canvas in the silent studio, he found his thoughts returning to her. Thoughts about what? There was nothing to remember, no physical sweetness distilled to memories as yet. What kept distracting him were the unknown events of his intended visit. She was like a dream stuck at its unfulfilled climax of pleasure. He knew the solution: he had to get away from himself right now, had to visit one of his senior peers in the adjoining building. He locked his door, walked along the long empty hallway past the closed doors of other studios, and went down the old creaking wooden stairway of what apparently had once been an old mill on the waterfront. He walked over the rough uneven earth and out the huge doorway, unto the sunken cobble stones of a street that was more than a century old, when wagons and buckboards drew up outside the blackened brick building that now faced a swirl of raised highway ramps along the nearby lakeshore.

He caught a freight elevator with two UPS men in their brown uniforms transporting three large paintings wrapped in plastic up to the artist's studio he was about to visit. The artist's studio door was wide open and he could hear his fists in rapid succession pounding a punching bag suspended from the ceiling.

"Heyyyyy Jerry, what's up?" Not waiting on a reply, the artist in his next sentence told the UPS men where to lean his returned canvasses, then after they were alone, the studio door shut, walked over to three cane chairs beside the long make-shift tables on wooden horses laden with all sorts of items necessary to their profession.

He moved off from contemplating the multi-layered, faintly dripping ground of various greens in one of the painter's unfinished canvases against the screen-wall at the center of the cleared studio floor. The arena where hand to surface combat took place.

"I was just idling over there man, came by to see what you're up to," he said.

"I'm fried," the older painter said, looking very relaxed, leaning back in his wrinkled check working shirt, his well-trimmed grey moustache complimenting his heavy grey hair combed back beside his ears and down to the top of his shoulders. "My show closed last week in Chicago, those were three returns from ten large works I showed."

He could never figure out if the painter's features were Jewish, Arab, French, or Eastern European (and never asked), even though he had a French-sounding surname. "I can't decide if the hardest part is beginning something fresh or just continuing," he said to the painter, and realized it sounded too much like something other than painting. A person, for instance. He knew whom.

"Want a cold Carlsberg? I'm having one," his host said, as he got up and went over to the small brown icebox and brought out two beers. "Did you do those push-ups before working, that I told you about? That helps you to relax. I also do Tai Chi." The older painter added.

"I didn't do any today; I sort of came into the studio in a distracted mood." He was tempted to go on about his recent encounter with Sonia, but his host cut in again.

"By the way," he said, "I've got something for you. I have a friend who just opened a spacious café on Peter Street. I've told him about you, so why don't you roll up about six of your canvasses and swing over there around 6.30 this evening, and see if you can decide on a date for a show?"

Out of the question! But he didn't say that. Couldn't, except think that was just his luck! In fact, he wasn't going to say anything about Sonia. How he had met her on his way into his studio this morning, or any of the other details. He couldn't appear not to be eagerly serious to get somewhere in this precarious business of being an artist! Not to Claude anyway, whose support in the art world could mean eventual success.

"Just what I probably needed to get back to some work," he lied, eager now to get out of Claude's studio before their conversation became too revealing. "Thanks a lot man, I'll check this guy out tonight."

"Good luck Jerry, I gotta get back to that ground anyways. Let me know how it goes, ok?"

As he went out, even before the artist's door clicked in its smooth well-used lock, he could hear Claude breathing hard as he began rapid push-ups which he knew lightened his hands prior to painting.

In his studio he felt more tension now that he had to decide whether to keep his 6 o'clock date with Sonia, or just abandon it for the audition that could boost his career and pocketbook. Half an hour wasn't much time to spend with Sonia, and the thing is she couldn't be reached because he hadn't asked for her number, and she didn't offer it. Probably just out of forgetfulness and humble confidence that he would turn up anyway. Actually, both opportunities were an achievement for one day, he thought, while pulling out a roll of eight 4 + 4 ft. canvasses and choosing six in the style he was at present pursuing. After rolling up his selection for the audition, he went back to his unfinished painting that was influenced by weather-beaten natural and fabricated material associated with the pre-historic Americas.

At around 1pm he left for a take-out Genoa salami sandwich and a V8 juice on King Street, came back in and ate while studying what he had accomplished so far, making a mental note of color combinations that could work. He turned on his transistor to Jazz FM91, and caught Carol Wellman doing "Hey Goodlookin,' What You Got Cooking?," Connie Roswell's version of Ellington's, "I Let A Song Go Out of My Heart," Alicia Pellman with "After You're Gone," Dianne Schorr's, "Midnight," Earl Hines Big Band's, "Swinging On Scene," all in a row, as he looked through his Dell editions of Turok, Son Of Stone, Sugarfoot, Maverick, Bat Masterson, Tales Of Wells Fargo, Lawman, Tonto, and finally Tubby & Lulu comic books.

He must have dozed off in his low-down easy chair, because when he looked at the time it was near four pm. He locked up, walked down Sherbourne to Queen and caught a Street Car west to McCaul where he had a ground floor Bay window front room in an old house. He had the six canvasses with him of course. First he gaffed in the kitchen with two guys who lived on the second floor. Then he took a warm shower, put on his pin-striped Le Chateau slacks with the wrinkled look, his black & white horizontal-striped t-shirt, splashed on some Iquitos— Alain Delon's Amazonian fragrance—then grabbed his sleek grey-brown trench coat. He gave up thinking about how the two appointments would turn out. Better said than done of course; but walking down Baldwin to Spadina where he caught a Street Car to the Subway about five corners north, he left any future decisions to the unknown. He walked down Spadina Road from the Subway, turned left on the corner of Lowther Avenue, then up the short way to Walmer Road that wound around a little island park.

When he reached the little zig-zag corner which began Kendall Avenue he realized he had walked back into a past he had not thought about for years. He realized then that if that past had been mostly pleasant he might have thought about it. He walked into a street of tall trees—they hadn't changed—which he knew went all the way to a major street in the distance, and it was as if their rustling heads above parked cars were showering him with scenes where he, alone or with his young wife, had rushed in and out of front doors, ran up stairs, turned corners at a pace influenced by beer, wine, pot, freezing wind, and snowflakes. When they once hurried up to bed and stayed there as Charlie Parker's "Night in Tunisia," and other favorite selections from the pile of jazz albums on a shelf beside them, played.

He stood on the clean quiet pave, like it had always been, and stared up at vines climbing outside the shut garret windows of the apartment where he had sat one summer afternoon writing an essay on some poet or painter, watching the walkway below to see when she would hurry home to the supper he had prepared.

He wondered how far away Sonia's house would be, and when he looked across the street, to a small white two-storied building with a wide clean driveway beside it, he recognized the address she had given. He walked across the street like someone who was idle, lazy, or had nowhere to go. Sonia appeared at the front door of a bottom flat in a deep purple bathrobe, her hair wet as she swept it back with her left hand while calling out his name. He went up two steps to a higher paved walkway across a small mown lawn before her house.

"Was it easy to find me?" she said.

He was thinking of his ex-wife at the window in the enclosed garret veranda behind him, on a slightly lower level than the floor of the one large room that had been their bedroom and salon. "Yes. I never memorized this number, but I knew the house." What he said didn't seem to make sense to him, and he kept hearing his words echoing in his mind.

"Did you live close by?" Sonia asked, after he had stepped inside, slipping off his canvas espadrilles while she shut the inner door behind him.

"No, not really, further up the street, past the park." Why did he lie? Anyway, there was no time for an analysis now.

"I thought you mistook my place for the one across the street; you seemed to want to go in there," she said.

So she did see him? "Well, that was a house I always wondered about. It dosen't look like it's changed at all." What was he after with all these lies? She noticed the roll of canvasses in his left hand as they entered the long salon with a couch, two easy chairs, and a small oriental carpet under a low coffee table, a vase with fresh sunflowers at the table's center, a few issues of Vogue, and a glossy coffee table book on contemporary fashion designers titled: Birds Of Paradise .

"Did you bring your work to show me?" she asked, with a

tone that he felt wasn't serious. But her question had serious implications, obviously, since he wasn't prepared to admit as yet that he had to leave shortly.

"You want to see them? Sure." That wasn't an answer, but he knew it was too awkward for her to demand a definitive reply.

"Ok, but make yourself comfortable, let me get you an Old Vienna. You like OV, don't you?" She didn't wait for an answer, "I do" she said, on her way to what was surely the kitchen down the salon hall, behind a partition with a small square opening, no doubt for communication with the salon. "I really should tidy up," she said, vanishing into a bedroom with her beer.

He had arrived a bit early, it was now approaching 6 pm, in twenty minutes he would have to leave, catch a bus down Spadina, come off at Phoebe, and walk a corner or so over to the café and audition. She returned in an orange toned silk Japanese kimono with willows and flowers and streams swirling all over it. While sipping her beer she blow-dried her hair, sitting on a vanity bench before a mirror above a narrow oak desk in the salon. Her body made itself curvaceous in profile from his position on an easy chair. In the silence that fell he found himself back in a house he had first lived in on her street, a house he knew stood about three doors down from hers on the same hand. He saw himself in its second floor front room with big curving bay windows, where in Spring budding tree branches grazed the glass panes, and in Summer leaves became shadows on the walls of his room from sunlight or street-light. He saw himself lying in his big bed, with Jimi Hendrix 'smoking' in the poster behind him on the wall, staring at the center of the mantle of the disused fireplace where a small bronze Buddha in lotus meditation, flanked by two small brass flutes with burning sticks of incense, faced him.

"You're quiet," she said, turning to face him from the bench, the two halves of her kimono falling away, revealing all her broad firm thighs before she crossed them.

"You want to see the pictures?" he said, unrolling them at her feet. It was a way to occupy her while he held on to the memory of someone, another girl. Maybe it was the similarity of the patterns on her Kimono that made him recall a dark voluptuous Oriental girl whom he had made love to once in a house down the street across the park, but had failed to on another occasion, when she had let him massage her bulging Venus mound through the silky floral psychedelic slacks she wore that early Summer afternoon, then left him half-naked on the floor of her bedroom with an erection.

"These are so gripping!" Sonia was saying, lifting one canvas after another. "Their brushstrokes are so swift and vigorous, yet precise!" she said.

It was a good time to tell her: "Sonia, I actually have to leave in about five minutes for an audition." Yet he had not one thought about that when he said it, but was seeing only his big bay room on the second floor of the house down the street, with the Oriental landlord who liked him when he had first answered the room for rent sign taped to a pillar on the front porch, directly beneath what would become his room. In their initial conversation he had spoken of his love for Basmattie rice, prawn Balchow, and how he had read a lot of Tagore and Krisnamurti.

"Oh my God, and you still came to see me!" Sonia was saying, while he was getting accustomed to what seemed to be her ironic replies. It was a magnetic escape remembering that Fall night when his friends—the English drummer of a Rock band whose first album was climbing the charts, and the slim cool blond singer with a smooth flexible feminine physique, who had released a hard driving ecstatic first album—arrived at his door with three groupies: a buxom English girl in a long velvet dress; a dark-haired girl from Quebec who looked like Anna Karina in Live Your Life, with the same short hairstyle, glove-tight black shirt and trousers against her milky skin; and a fast-talking French Moroccan girl with shoulder length Henna red hair, Roman sandals, and a floral silk dress buttoned right down the front. The beer-crazy drummer held a twenty-four case of Export beer against his waist circled by a broad black belt decorated with silver conchos. He remembered they listened to the Yarbirds, Cream, Traffic, Hendrix, Free, and Santana, as they spoke of Baudelaire's and Nietzsche's adventures, the aroma and blue smoke of tobacco and hashish wafting in the room's shadowy interior and the cool beer soothing their throats. He remembered the tree branches trembling and rubbing the window panes like human fingers when they made love across the big bed and on the carpet, almost laughing at each-other's boldness in the dark, the perfume of the girls transferred to their skins when they exchanged partners. He remembered hearing their sedated voices on the deserted sidewalk below his room as they made their way back in the cool night to an exclusive apartment building just up the street, after which he fell into a deep sleep, and woke up with the glow of sunlight filling the bay windows, and the Moroccan girl still asleep beside him.

"I said I would, but not for how long," he found himself saying after it seemed ages had passed. It was the best excuse he could muster on the spot, thinking of when he awoke each morning in that bay room and there was nothing to run off to; no auditions, no anxiety about being late anywhere, only the articles he wrote each week for the Underground Press, and the commissions from the paintings he sold for the company founded by the Rock musicians who were his friends down the street.

"You see why I like being down around the Queen Street

scene?" She said. He saw, nodding as though trying to dismiss something buzzing around inside his head. "I bet you're hurrying off back down there," she said, picking up her glass of beer from the coffee table and taking some huge gulps.

What he was trying to get away from was actually the same house a few doors down, but not the same bay room, rather a more reclusive small attic one above, where, married, he had returned with his young wife after their foreign travels and ended up right back at the same address. Sonia, who had stood up when he did, said; "It's getting a bit nippy out, isn't it?" He was backing a window whose mesh was half raised. She came up to him and held out his trench coat. He could smell the fragrance of her freshly washed hair, yet simultaneously saw the face of his young wife behind his back, staring from across the street through a window in the garret which they had rented after moving from the attic room close by. He heard her scream one morning, after a night of hectic gallivanting—eating out with friends, returning home late tipsy on wine, making love straight away. They had forgotten Lasagna under foil out on the cold stove for a few days, and that morning, raising the foil, she had discovered the Lasagna swarming with maggots. Next he saw his fresh blood curling in the lavatory bowl in that apartment across the street, and felt the shooting pain of his anal muscles contracting like needling fireworks after having hemaroid surgery...

He pecked Sonia on her lips that seemed to wait before him. "I don't have your number," he said.

"I'm such an air-head sometimes," she said laughing, and hurried off to her bedroom, returning with her business card, work address, number, and personal phone number on it. They walked to the edge of the pave, he with the roll of canvas under his right arm, she hugging herself across her prominent chest.

"I'll call," he said, then took off at a pace like a man fleeing a crime, aware that he had seen light inside the garret-apartment across the street, where nothing seemed to stir.

He caught a Spadina bus south, arriving at the upstairs café about fifteen minutes to seven. The owner was a short Chinese man dressed in white drill trousers and a white shirt with buttoned down pockets, like a Customs official. He wore little round glasses in metal frames, and his hair was cut short, carefully brushed to either side of a part at the center of his little head. The walls of the café were painted in a faint pastel pink, the tables and chairs in pastel turquoise, the concrete floor, carmine. "Yes, Claude said to expect you," the little man said with a faint smile, standing up before a table and mentioning his name. There were about three pairs of male customers at tables well apart; it was a big café. He rolled out the works on the table between them. He could tell by the look on the man's face that he was surprised, but not in a positive way. "It's a little strong for my taste, and a little unusual for what I had in mind; but there's always changes in artists' works, aren't they? Let's get together again sometime." He thought they both knew that wasn't going to happen.

He didn't have to walk far, just around a few bends, to arrive at McCaul Street. It was a relief to rush across the old porch, through the front door that was never locked, into the big front room with high ceilings, a huge old defunct fireplace, and his bed in a far corner of the floor which the morning light illuminated after passing over a round café table and two folding chairs beside the bay window with a view across the porch, garden, and quiet street. He dropped his paintings into an easy chair and went down the hallway to the kitchen.

"Fried potatoes gentlemen, coffee?" The red-haired Scottish drifter and surfer who knew Hollywood, Big Sur, Vancouver,

Honolulu, asked before the stove. There were fried Tofu slabs on plates, a bottle of black Chinese sauce to go with it, and a big bowl of mixed nuts on the dining table. The bearded long-haired Gypsy student of philosophy appeared at the door of a back room with a couch and two easy chairs before a TV, nothing more, except the glimpse of trees in the backyard beside the old flaking white-washed garage in the alleyway.

"Grab your grub guys and get it quick, here he comes!" the student said, laughing. They grabbed some plates of Tofu with forks and flopped down on the couch before the TV where Dr. No had just begun.

On the screen a beautiful lady was writing a check, her voice asking to whom she should sign it; then Sean Connery's cuff-linked hands appear, lifting a cigarette out of its case, placing it at the side of his thin lips, then adding his lighter's flame to it, smoke beginning to stream through his nostrils, before he said: "Bond, James Bond."

"Pass the nuts," the artist said, a big grin on his face.

COLORED SPAGHETTI

If Claude thought he was ok to be around, then he must be. That's what she thought the first time she set eyes on him over at Claude's big studio, with its two long rows of dust-coated radiators hissing below big windows covered in sheets of plastic. The windows faced a freeway along the lakeshore where a few big ships' funnels could be seen. Around them in the studio were an old couch, a bicycle, a punching bag, a drum-kit, and all sorts of cartons, plastic wrappers, torn posters, etc, which the factory warehouses in the area threw out, and which Claude collected, arranged, pasted and painted upon. These works were eventually consigned to art gallery walls across Canada and the USA, from where they vanished into so many homes, businesses, institutions, for sums no one would have guessed such disposable material could be creatively recycled into.

Well, she figured it was magic those patrons were really paying for. Not the kind shown on TV with puffs of colored smoke and obvious tricks of course, but what Claude, her teacher of experimental painting in the class she attended at Art College, spoke about as the pleasures of animism and fetishism embedded in original African, South American, North American, and South Seas cultures.

So there they were in Claude's studio one winter afternoon after she had visited a friend nearby in hers. They were introduced, that was all, so she couldn't really be sure about anything, except that he was one of those mixed-blood colored

52

guys, though not an American or Canadian. She had been close enough to them in Clubs, on TV screens, in transit, or on the street, to know his accent wasn't theirs. If he had any accent at all, really, except what proved to be a definitive knowledge of English, in the sense of an intellectual vocabulary, mixed with those standard subculture words and phrases like 'checkout', 'later', 'cool', 'heavy', 'sure thing', 'I bet', 'big on you' etc, they all used.

What had her laughing like some coquettish playmate who had little worthwhile to contribute to the way-out conversation between the two artists, was Claude's poker-faced rendition of baby elephants toddling down the sidewalks of Calcutta, or people without arms or feet sliding by on balls of flesh; then the colored guy, when not making some point about Montaigne's essay on Cannibals, or Rousseau's 'Noble Savage', or Sir Thomas More's 'Utopia', was relating anecdotes about the amazing Native Indian art installations he liked in old technicolor Westerns like: She Wore A Yellow Ribbon, Taza Son of Cochise, Drums Across the River, Comanche Station, which he found inspirational. And all the while Claude would have this sly haughty look on his face with its pencil-grey moustache below his aquiline nose, giving her side glances as though he were one of those snobbish butlers in certain old black and white 1930's movies she had seen. As though they were talking for her benefit. As though neither of them could care less whether she had chosen her tight green fatigues and black cashmere sweater that made her breasts look like a pair of bayonet bulbs, because she had a crush on Claude. After all she was just a well-off kid from Montreal (her father was French and a doctor, and mother an Italian boutique owner on St Catherine Street) who, continually hearing of some New Wave art scene that had taken off in Toronto, had pestered her parents to pay for a three-year course in experimental painting, and a small apartment down the same street of the Art College she attended.

So now it's a month later, in Spring, and she isn't the kind of girl to go unnoticed, so apart from all the phone numbers, addresses, and invitations to studio parties pinned to a cork board in her big one room apartment, what made her both noticeable and popular—apart from her tall wide-hipped elegant walk and slim Elizabeth Taylor-like features—was the way she had become familiar in the cafes, the bars, restaurants, boutiques, music, art, and book stores, and of course art galleries on Queen St. The way she sauntered down the sidewalks, her head of teased-out spiked hair dyed a mixture of gold and carmine above her long slender swan's neck turning this way and that with her royal gaze shaped by classic molds as old as Rome and Judea, stopping to window shop, unaware—or as though unaware—once, that the weird colored guy she had met over at Claude's studio was coming up beside the window in her direction. So because she had seen his reflection in the huge pane, or just happened to look his way, they met again. It was then she remembered hearing his name before they first met. This was among art students who were arguing about the articles he had written on films and painters. So she asked him about all this, and he took her into a bookstore to pick up a copy of a subsidized art journal, where she saw his essay just published on Claude's work. And that's how he ended up giving her the paperback edition of Levi-Strauss's Tristes Tropiques which he held in his hand along with a few other books and magazines.

When they parted after walking to Spadina and Queen, he had in his possession her address and phone number scribbled on a small page torn out of her spiral-bound notebook. He had capriciously thought of her as "Georgy Girl," from that decades-old song, when sighting her that day window shopping. By the time he paid his first visit to her apartment and found her, along with two girl-friends from distant small towns pursuing careers in Toronto, listening to albums by Pat Benitar, Brian Ferry, Carol Pope, Steely Dan, and Chic, he realized she hadn't a clue how someone like him, with interests like his, or theirs, had come to exist. Even before the topic turned to their various backgrounds elsewhere, he had perceived her sly caution towards such a conversation, as though it really didn't matter where he came from, when in fact it did, not in a negative, but, even more compelling, in a secretive way, since at the mention of the name British Guiana, where he was old enough to have been born before it achieved its post-colonial name of Guyana, her face had remained blank, reflecting only faint recollections in Canadian newspaper tidbits about mostly Orientals struggling to become Canadian or American immigrants. But one of her girlfriends did mention some famous waterfall, and the film To Sir With Love, with Sidney Poitier as the black Guyanese immigrant teacher in a white English ghetto school, which she had heard of but never seen. This suggesting some obscure tradition behind the bearded, curly-headed colored guy sitting among them in his dark crimson collarless disco shirt, chicly tapered chocolate brown slacks with cuffed bottoms over brass buckles on his grey leather boots.

Were they going to be just friends, or was there something she wanted, and he wanted, which only time could reveal? He imagined she must have wondered why his behavior was so familiar, so free of any special awareness of a privilege or opportunity attributed to their company. At times in conversations she seemed to hint that they, whatever their race or origin, comprised a separate class created by Art, but he got the impression that was just a convenient mask to satisfy the still nagging question of his unruffled disposition before her and her girlfriends, even when they sometimes frankly exposed their personal toilette and wildly explicit vulgar behavior in anecdotes.

Yet he never disclosed to her and her girlfriends, or her apparent white boyfriends encountered a few times, the memories which somehow flowed through his mind in the midst of their company: The suddenly returning sound of high heels tapping across the polished wooden floorboards of his white wooden house with green banisters and lozenge Venetian relief designs on its outer wall and front door, opened by dented gleaming brass knobs; the fragranced trail off the black glossy hairstyle, like Susan Pleschette's in one of her recent films, of his sisters' Syrian girlfriend whose striped peddle-pushers he once heard being peeled down in their washroom, followed by the rushing sound of her urine in the bowl, which somehow sounded extraordinary to his ten-year-old ears, provoking imaginary descriptions about the look and density of its exit; their lip-stick mouths chewing bubble-gum, and shrill voices between laughter as they rushed down the front stairs, his mother's last cautionary remarks from the drawing room yelled back to with reassurance, then their ticking silver and cream ladies bicycles wheeled out under the blazing blue tropical afternoon sky with wispy white clouds, as the sea-side backyard wash fluttered in the tide's breeze. The weekly cosmopolitan house fetes where girls of Dutch, Flemish, German, French, Amerindian, African, Portuguese, Irish, Scottish, English, Italian/Maltese, Danish, Swedish, Swiss, Chinese, East Indian, extraction and lineage, including all their now obscure mixed descent, sat around the drawing room walls in upright chairs, their small uncapped bottles of Lime Rickey and Vimto aerated pop smoking piquant gassy vapor around their straws; his first time comparing and appreciating female legs exposed by skirts and dresses in dazzling colors, of various breath and length on local models of fashion, whose attitudes and behavior somehow seemed influenced by the screen roles of Nathalie Wood, Ava Gardner, Jane Russell, Dorothy Dandridge, Jennifer Jones, Audrey Hepburn, Sophia Loren, Elizabeth Taylor, Lee Remick, Bridgette Bardot, Silvana Mangano, Jean Seberg, Elke Sommer, or Julie Christie. The sudden death of popular beauties, local models, socialite and party girls—whose faces and figures graced weekly pages in the four Dailies—from botched abortions; or, on a number of occasions, after the wild gay newspaper photos on the 'Society' page of marriage to some stationed Data Control American serviceman in the Capital, prior to departure for the USA, the opposite news in a fortnight of their death in a sports car smash-up.

The naïve innocence of her lack of exclusivity while in the company of his mute experiences only added to her attractiveness in his eyes. It was all the same, he often thought, this continuity of lifestyles on the edge of social convention he had emigrated to become part of. These sudden phone calls from his Toronto artist peers, male or female, announcing the unlikely event of a snowfall in the middle of summer; sometimes crammed into the back seat of cars, the night's female catch sitting on his lap as the foamy remains in a champagne bottle went around; the distance between one studio party and the next somewhere at the end of a dark maze of corners traversed wildly, an inebriated voyage accomplished by luck and chance; no less hasty than those made blazing along the lights of a highway to greet some artist returning a 'success' from Europe at the airport; or musician from another rising New Wave group's hectic tour. This at a time when guitars riffed like scraped tin, stripes were in, and hungry stars fell among them like snowflakes; when fuschia-pink reigned and obscure brushstrokes evoking Oceanic carvings and antique Amazonian designs appeared disguised on gallery walls.

While among them he carried within him the ghostly faces

of other youths far away—no less white, blonde, dark-haired or
freckled like her friends, but most of all with temperaments at once
attractive, bold, caring, and adored—seventeen year-old college
prefects seen in their glove-tight bleached demin Wranglers and
striped Bossa Nova shirts, soft Banlon jerseys, continental slacks
and fibre espadrilles, parking their Triumphs, Husqvarnas, and
Hondas under the matinee marquees of cinemas showing their
favorite films, like: The Devil's Hairpin with Cornel Wilde,
All the Fine Young Cannibals with Robert Wagner, The Gene
Krupa Story with Sal Minoe, Rebel Without a Cause with James
Dean, The Subterraneans with George Peppard, Written on the
Wind with Robert Stack, A Man and a Woman with Jean-Louis
Trintignant, etc. Such influences perhaps later unconsciously
condensed into one fatal flaw, when, after one of those sumptuous
house fetes, the young motorcyclist stuffed with spiced minced
meat and green-pea patties, crab-backs, chicken chowmein, black
pudding with pepper sauce, all chased with the addictive mixture
of Russian Bear rum and ginger ale, and perhaps those few but
treacherously effective glasses of Rum Punch, already anxious
to open up along one of those long straight coastal roads almost
deserted in the dead of night (the left-over dams of old Demerara
plantations turned roadways barely illuminated by canting old
lamp-posts), full throttle, bent over the warm intoxicating aroma
oozing off the trembling gasoline tank, somehow totally forgets
the multiplied inebriated effect of a soothing sea breeze flowing
over adjacent sports fields, and the seawall less than half a mile
away, until in that deadly half-minute of nodding sleep the road
ending at a junction is overshot, and what is discovered by a more
fortunate late-night person are the remains of a once beautiful
face and head smashed to a pulp like a ripe watermelon against
two bound telephone poles.

Or, once more helmet-less (in those days), instinctively

swerving to avoid a night-hunting cat, is knocked unconscious to the head by the rail of a wooden bridge to a sports club and discovered floating drowned, face down at dawn beside his half-submerged Triumph in the peaceful orange ripples of a canal two centuries old, which once irrigated a vanished sugar plantation.

He never related any of this as his contribution to their conversations. Nor the courtship forbidden by his parents of one of his popular sisters to a distant relative, one of the wild motorcyclists, different by his creole European blonde features, but not by the family blood they shared. Or his father's painful decision to reject an offer of marriage to another of his sisters, whose white Data Control American boyfriend could not produce the letter of acceptance from his parents which his father demanded. He remembered the day of this traumatic revelation for the young quiet Montgomery Clift type American serviceman, who afterwards lay sedated in his clean khaki uniform with matching canvas belt across his parents' big bed, as he gazed at him in twelve-year-old sympathy from the bedroom door. How could he relate any of this to her circle? It would have sounded like the very desire to prove his social compatibility, which he knew was unnecessary, or redundant on his part.

And then he vanished. Or rather, he hadn't been seen for a few weeks, on those afternoons or nights their crowd walked out dressed attractively, looking for, yet saying they were surprised when they found each-other on the sidewalks along that old Royal city street now taken over by their wealthier peers, who had introduced bookstores, music stores, art galleries, boutiques, cafes, and all sorts of special outlets that no one seemed to think could be stores in the past. A rumor surfaced that he had been hospitalized. So where was he now? She was silently astonished when none of her peers, who also knew him, seemed to consider that being alone at such a time was not particularly as enjoyable as the social activity they continued to enjoy each week or day without him. She found out the location of his studio from Claude, who had spoken to him by phone, and she decided to go over unannounced. She shopped for some groceries she thought would do him good, such as Maramite, Soya milk, almond and apple butter, and a few pounds of crunchy granola.

As the hour, just after 1pm, approached on the day set aside for her visit, the idea came to her to present herself in a most noticeable fashion. She teased out her Roman helmet of cerise hair, pulled on a tight flame-orange low-neck jersey which highlighted her braless bosom like two jugs of cream in the process of being spilled. Her skirt was a light tie-dyed cotton affair of pleated lime green, pink, and purple. It was short and flounced like certain of those college girl uniforms in private upper-class schools. Her see-through pure acrylic high heels made a sharp determined sound after she had slammed her apartment door and swayed down the hallway. She broke into mild absurd laughter when she recalled an old European black and white film where beautiful Jewish women, well fed and nourished in a Nazi concentration camp, were striped naked by obsessed Third Reich experimental doctors and made to embrace the warmth of their breasts, stomach, and thighs upon old dying male Jewish prisoners, gasping for breath, while serious, dedicated experimental Nazi doctors in their white lab coats, timed the extension of life provided by this exercise of sensual warmth upon hopelessly expiring male bodies.

His studio was an old defunct storefront on a side-street in the clean, quiet, garment district. It was part of a row of similar defunct old stores rented cheaply to artists. He had dropped an Oriental cane curtain over a large glass window where the faded red letters of a past Portuguese garment business were still partly visible. She went up a few concrete steps from the sidewalk and knocked on the wooden green door with a rusted metal letter slot. She heard slow movements across a wooden floor before his face appeared quickly at the side of the lifted bamboo curtain. She heard an inner door then the one before her open, and he stood in the three or four feet space between each door where there were a snow shovel, an old broom, and winter boots on a mat. He was leaning on one of those do-it-yourself stretchers, like wounded, hatless Randolph Scott limping with the aid of a Winchester out a gold mine at the end of Seven Men From Now.

"Look who's here!" He said, as though speaking to someone else present but unknown to her.

"How have you been Roland? Claude said you were hospitalized."

"They took out my appendix. Come in woman."

"Oh, that's awful! I brought you this." She said.

He looked at her plastic shopping bag and smiled. "You're going to make a good wife someday Jenny, sit down."

"To who? Is your friend Claude married?" She sat down in one low easy chair before a large unpainted wooden work table about one foot off the faded cheap carpet on a floor painted a thick glossy grey.

"So you're in love with your teacher. What's new?"

"Who says I'm in love? I might just want a rich artist!"

"Well welcome to the girls club, but you're late."

"You mean he's already married, but not for love?"

"Is that what I mean? Ok, so that seems to leave his love interests open, and you can now admit you're in love with your teacher."

She laughed. And while he offered her a glass of chilled crackling Mateus Rose, then limped off leaning on his stretcher to get it, she took in the quiet effect of the bare white walls with light blue base boards, the room's blank enclosure broken by three sizes of bright paintings leaning three or four together, which had caught her eye from the moment she stepped into the room. Now there was no mistaking the floating colored spaghetti-like lines, creating unorthodox order; the carmine balls that were nothing more than a large paint-coated brush spun by his wrist (she got up to inspect) seeming to advance or recede in their spatial grounds like movement in a 3-D film; the wobbling zig-zag borders that traversed the length and breath of canvasses, and within which rings of silver fell like raindrops on grounds of dark creeping carmine, dust-like ochre, or stark white sunlight.

He came back slowly with their two glasses filled with chilled wine, his stick left somewhere she could see was partitioned into a small kitchen beside a bedroom with large sash windows, and a back door no doubt leading to a verdant backyard and alleyway. As he leaned to offer her glass he sighed with the effect of pain, but at the same time could not help noticing how, due to the low position of his easy chair she sat in and her generous height (she was a good foot taller than him), her loose colorful skirt fell away from her knees drawn up together, so that the roundness of her thighs and bare hips traversed diagonally by the edges of her panties were revealed, leaving that precious valley below her belly concealed by the posture of her elevated insteps and heels within the straps across her crystal clear transparent acrylic stilettos.

He wondered if she was aware of her posture, or if she had merely dismissed his masculinity as harmless due to his physical state? Whatever, he was titillated enough to have a smile on his face as he chose an LP and put it on the stereo kept in a corner of the room. As the first waves of sound rose he moved one large canvas off another so that side by side they revealed their leaping shapes and rippling lines against the white wall.

"That's the theme from The Good the Bad and the Ugly, right?"

"You mean the music or the painting?"

"Both," she said, after a moment of thought.

"Good," he said. "I like Westerns with Indian blankets, arrows, lances, shields, ponchos, white-washed abode walls, and so on; also instrumental music like that trumpet you're hearing now in Morricone's theme."

"You're nuts Roland, so is Claude!"

"Isn't that nice," he said flatly.

"I'm so glad I met you guys!"

And for the next hour they spoke of Kandinsky's Concerning the Spiritual in Art, which she was reading at present; the avant-garde abstract designs of Russian Constructivist painters like Popova and Exter; of Levi-Strauss's Tristes Tropiques, the off-beat geometric face tattoos of the Caduevo tribe of Brazil, and other structures of art by South American Indians.

He didn't see her for another month. By that time he had recuperated enough to attend a party at Claude's studio after the opening of another one of his exhibitions, where the center of each painting on display was the only area of vivid activity in an expanse of space like dripping chlorophyll, or rawhide bleaching in harsh sunlight, or the blue indigo of some cosmic twilight, or.....

He was thinking of her while acting briefly as the party's DJ, and put on Wayne Shorter's "Elegant People" from Black Market that night when she stood out in the crowd, both of them draining their champagne glasses over their smiles locked in silent knowledge of something unspoken across the crowded buzzing studio floor.

On another night at a loft party on Spadina near King he had arrived late, already elevated with sex she thought, since he had that red head with him, the restaurant owner from some old European aristocratic family whom everyone seemed to know. Through a slightly ajar bedroom door where she lay

back on a bed in her underwear within a nest of other semi-
nude girls, languid with Southern Comfort mixed with white
bubbly Spumante, prepared for whatever lay in store later that
night, she had seen him in the crowd that stood in small circles
lifting their paper cups to their lips or digging into the Halva
and Pate while their bodies vibrated to the throbbing demo-
tape of a visiting English New Wave band on the rise. She
wondered if he felt as different as he seemed to her: someone
whose ideas on art, film, music, led to arguments. Her very
thoughts confirmed later when she heard from the party's host
(they were celebrating his recently awarded Canada Council
B-Grant) how the leader of the British Pop group, aware of his
colonial origin, and popularity in an intellectual field which
no doubt seemed to escape some old colonial bond the young
British musician was still naïve enough to believe they had in
common, strode up to him and said, as though they were already
in the midst of a familiar conversation that had begun centuries
ago: "Look, I'm tired of you blokes beating us at cricket!" And
he had replied calmly, without hesitation: "Listen, I don't give a
fuck about your cricket." The host said the crowd around them
had dispersed instantly with bowed heads, choking on their
drinks and laughter. That night she had whispered, "Roland!
Roland!", as he went by the slightly ajar bedroom door, but he
didn't seem to hear or notice her…or maybe that woman with
him was close by? "And what would you have done if he had
come in?" One of her girlfriends later asked. "What do you
think!" She said, loudly.

Some might have called it an obsession if they knew she
wanted to sit in a bar on Queen Street expecting him to walk
by in his cream Sir James boots with white jeans stuck into the
top, a soft long rust-colored Oriental scarf wrapped twice around
his neck inside the upturned collar of his sports jacket, and one

of those Crème de la Crème little cigars smoking between his fingers. And she did sit at two or three bars around two in the afternoon when she knew he left his studio and came down Queen looking into the comic-book stores. One time he did see her behind a big store-front window with her legs crossed on a stool at one of the bars, and all she did was point between them to the full glass of white wine at the end of the bar, and he came in and drank it, standing up, his boots on the brass rest, yet not a word between them, while she kept hearing the theme from The Good the Bad and the Ugly in her wine-stewed mind.

One afternoon when she hadn't been on the street at one of those bars, there was a knock at her door. She was expecting an upcoming artist she had recently started dating, but Roland stood there instead. She opened the door wide and let him in, neither of them saying a word. She could see he'd had a few glasses of wine already. She was in her silk mauve brasserie and matching panties. She walked away to the right of her bed, which was facing the door, and put an LP on the stereo. It was Morricone's theme from The Good the Bad and the Ugly. Roland had remained bracing the door after it was shut. She walked back to him as though going to the other end of the room. He held her calmly around her naked waist and said: "No more talk," then threw her on the bed. "What for?" she said calmly, smiling. Just then there was a slight knock on the door, then another. She sprung up, grabbed a skirt and T-shirt off a chair and pulled them on while Roland hurried silently around her bed and sat in a cane chair, crossing his legs. He picked up an 'Art Forum' from the carpet and spread it on his lap as she opened the door.

A tall good-looking young man with shoulder length brown hair said: "Hi!" and she said: "Eric, this is Roland, Roland, Eric," looking from one to the other. "We were just about to order spaghetti and meat balls." She said.

"Sounds good to me!" Eric said, as he walked over and sat on the cane couch under the large front window.

She glanced at Roland as she swayed over to the phone, smiling.

MEETING MABA

A man, a local white man, barefoot like his short squat Native Indian wife who always walked behind him, came to his family's East Street house in the city from time to time. A friend of his father, he and the man sat drinking some special home-made wine (brewed from potatoes, or corn, or pineapples) the couple always brought with them. His mother baked and served pastries while they drank, and the man always had stories to tell of his adventures far away in the jungle, forest, or savannah from which he returned maybe once a year to the city, and often visited their house on East Street with the big orange canal between its north and south one-way lanes.

Before the couple left his house the man's Indian wife, who usually said maybe three or four words throughout the whole visit, would always leave some small artifact of her culture: a tray made of woven palms; a boxed basket with a black inlaid geometric design; a long cylindrical woven container for the chemical creation of an indigenous concoction; a water jug and matching ladle made of red clay which kept water naturally cool, even though their household had a refrigerator. His mother hung these objects on a cream wall in the dining room, and the jug was placed on a western window sill shaded by a Venetian shutter held open by a stick.

Sometimes, idle and alone at the dining table, he contemplated these objects on the wall, went up close and removed them from their nails to stare at their intricately woven structural patterns.

By that time he was seven, which some say is the age of reason. This could explain why he began to make a connection between the Indian artifacts and utensils he also saw in Hollywood Westerns he loved—films like Broken Arrow, Across the Wide Missouri, Drums Across the River, The Far Horizons—and those that hung on the walls of the dining room. And yet he had no detailed knowledge of his country's 'interior' as yet, from where these objects and the quiet couple who brought them arrived, except he knew lengthy rivers, large and small, meandering creeks, dense jungles, high forests, savannahs, mountains, lakes, rocky plateaus, and waterfalls existed there.

Around his mid-teens, immersed in the hectic life of the Capital: attending weekend house fetes, dancing, obsessive cinema going, and very fashion-conscious, yet at the same time studying for GCE Exams, while avidly discovering the prose of Flaubert, Maupassant, Zola, Stendhal, Dostoyevsky, Goethe, Rousseau, Moravia, Pavese, Hemingway, Faulkner, Scott-Fitzgerald, and Carson McCullers, whose paperbacks lined his bookcase, he had almost completely forgotten the rustic couple who no longer came to his house. Or when they did he missed them, what with his teenage urban interests defined by rushing in and out the house, where the various artifact gifts of the native lady merely caught his eyes at a fleeting glance, instead of those prolonged moments of focused interest as before.

One moonlit night he came home exhilarated after seeing My Fair Lady for about the third time at the Astor cinema. He rode home in high spirits along Church Street, almost as if he were tipsy, sometimes leaning back from the M-shaped handlebars of his blue Raleigh bike, steering only with his rotating feet, feeling the nudge of sea-breeze from the seawall a little over a mile away when he crossed two-lane Camp Street with its tree-lined pedestrian avenue in the middle, similar to Thomas

Street at the next corner, where he turned left sharply in a zig-zag manner, his mind still hearing over and over that infectious song, "On the Street Where You Live", his favorite of the entire film, while seeing the lone gentleman singer strolling down the street singing. The scene that had brought him back to the cinema more than twice.

On Thomas Street he rode beside towering two-storied white wooden houses with their Venetian wooden shutters open at a diagonal by sticks, inviting the trade winds and sea breeze. He turned right, into Murray Street with its pavilion-like architectural styles and long verandas overhung with curved zinc awnings painted in weather-beaten pastel stripes. Making a left into East Street he rode the short distance up to his house facing east, with its red roof and one blooming tree of magenta flowers inside its fence, and front row of glazed crystal window panes which dimmed the powerful early morning sun. Without dismounting he stretched forward, noisily unlatched the metal gate and rode onto a concrete floor beneath the house raised on white stone pillars. He abandoned his bike with a clatter against the magenta-painted concrete enclosure of the front stairs.

Hanging out a big window at the side of the two-storied mansion next door was the head of a girl with thick black waves of hair. It was impossible to make out her face, yet they were perhaps no more than ten feet apart; she above him as he looked up from his clean empty bottom-house, his features no doubt quite visible to her, since the moon stood out high, huge, and crystal clear to the right of him, but to the left of her, casting her face in complete shadow. There was a sturdy six-feet high unpainted wooden fence between them, and on her side tall sunflowers, roses, hibiscus, and various other tropical plants were divided by a paved driveway for the family's blue Vauxhall parked in the lattice-work garage directly under where she stood at the window, since the house began at least a quarter of the way into the long yard. They said goodnight, and he commented on the brightness of the moon, adding quite absent-mindedly that he could see the map of North and South America reflected in the moon's surface. She said the moon was even brighter where she came from. And where was that he asked, realizing for the first time that she was from some distant region of the country, and no doubt of Native Indian origin. She told him she was from the North West, an area over two-hundred miles away adjacent to Venezuela, and from a town in the hills called Mabaruma. After he admitted he had heard of it, but never been there, they exchanged names, and hers she said was Maba.

Before he went up the back stairs to his house that night the memory of the barefoot hermit couple who had visited several times, returned to him with sudden renewed vigor. In the clarity of daylight, with the fresh scent of watered earth and flowers which rose between the slanted open sash windows of his bedroom and the vertical big open window where Maba had appeared the night before, he saw her again, confirmed as a Native Indian girl whose solid head of jet black wavy hair perhaps admitted just the touch of another race. She was sweeping the polished floor around large shining brass pots with blooming palms; coffee tables with small ferns under two pale blue arches; rocking and Morris chairs; a small old Grand Steinway piano and its bench at a diagonal in a corner near the opposite wall, beside another large window on the other side of the dining room.

Her employers' household was headed by a short jovial Oriental man, a businessman who wore white shorts, white shirts, and leather slippers, sat in a rocking chair (overlooking the driveway) offering a breezy view of the street corner just three mansions away; the best spot, some neighbors said, with a view to where wide Middle Street divided East Street. The businessman read magazines on 'sexology' while sipping Russian Bear rum from a gallon jug his wife purchased each week with the help of their teenage sons, the same age as he, their neighbor, who enjoyed coming for the drive down to a depot on Lombard Street, alongside the Demerara river with its wharves and the high bows and towering masts of international merchant ships.

Perhaps apart from the benevolent customs of his religion, the head of this neighborhood household, inspired by the jovial spirit this local rum produced in him, encouraged the almost weekly gift of a tray of hot Oriental cuisine: a bowl of chicken or mutton curry with side dishes of steamed greens and fried potatoes; a heap of rotis and puries; boiled 'channa' (chick peas) rolled in red pepper, garlic, and onion; all delivered by their new Native Indian servant girl to his parents' back door. Of course his parents, or rather his mother, returned these favors with selections of her cuisine: a tray of fruit cake, pine tarts, meat patties , and risoles, which he delivered. Like this the opportunity grew to know Maba.

His heart conflagrated like a match-head one day when she sent a message to him by one of the little boys of her household inviting him to turn on his transistor to share her favorite song, which was "My Girl" by Otis Redding. One day he returned her favor by the same boy inviting her to catch "Warm and Tender Love" by Percy Sledge, which was on the airwaves at present. The boy returned her message that she was already listening to it. It wasn't long before they began to meet secretly in a section of her employers' bottom-house enclosed in latticework walls, outside of which, along two fences, various tropical plants flourished. Sometimes they met in the wild backyard of banana, star-apple and breadfruit trees, among which stood the little unpainted wooden hut of an eccentric hermit Oriental caretaker.

At other times he embraced Maba as she leaned against a pillar enclosed by latticework beneath her employers' house, his hands on the nape of her neck, fingertips tracing her black glossy roller-coaster hair, the warmth of her belly felt through over-sized cast off skirts and blouses. Her perspiring face with features that sort of reminded him of Jane Russell, struck him as perfectly conducive to the vegetable scent of green onions, thyme, hot peppers and tomatoes clinging to her perspiring forehead, chest and arms, while her fingertips played with the short curls behind his neck. This entirely captured him romantically. Sometimes they met near noon in the wild backyard; those days when he attended only morning classes, then 1pm matinees at the huge white wooden Empire cinema palace just around the corner on Middle Street, and whose tall rear concrete wall was also one of her household's backyard fences.

They met beneath the smooth drooping shady green leaves of a banana tree upon whose soft trunk he had carved their initials in a heart. They whispered, kissed, and necked, after which he scaled the tall concrete fence and disappeared as she watched, dropping into the clean wide paved perimeter of the cinema's enclosed compound. He usually entered the stalls exhilarated, one time just as Audie Murphy in cinemascope was chased by a posse in the opening scenes of Ride a Crooked Trail.

Neither he nor Maba had thought a law they had vaguely heard of, which protected Native Indian girls (usually in domestic work) from urban exploitation and abuse, could apply to them. But when one of his love-letters to her was found on her employers' kitchen floor (she obviously carried it on her out of protection, or even to be re-read regularly), his parents and her (single) mother were informed. His mother went into hysterics, his father theatrics, thrusting one hand into a trouser pocket frenetically, in a gesture suggesting the financing of his marriage, to which he laughed and added they had no such intention, but were simply in love.

Forbidden to socialize, they now rarely saw each-other at close quarters, and never spoke. But one day walking home from college which was a few corners away, he heard distinct sobs and gasps as he neared his bridge, and realized it was coming from her employers' inner driveway next door. There Maba stood weeping profusely outside the garage door, while an older woman with her features, her mother, who had arrived in the city, brandished a half-charred piece of firewood. Her mother was yelling: "Tell me who is this …?" He heard his name mentioned as he walked up to her calmly, took the weapon out of her hand, and said to her startled face: "I'm the person you mentioned, and we don't settle problems that way here." At the spur of the moment he had actually felt glad to be influenced by that scene in Gunfight at the OK Corral, when un-armed Burt Lancaster as Marshall Wyatt Earp had taken a gun out of an inebriated cowboy's hand in a saloon.

A few days later, on a Saturday, Maba managed to send an oral message to him by one of her employers' little boys who had remained their faithful confidante. The message was that she was leaving by coastal steamer for her distant district later that very day. Staring through his bedroom window he saw her dressed in black skirt and blouse, lingering in the drawing room near the window of their first encounter. He sent back a message saying he would be dressed in black on the seaside promontory beside the river's mouth, which the ship had to pass as it departed the city. And he was, in the stark 2pm sun, leaning on the short narrow wall of the deserted promontory parallel to the river's mouth. He recognized her distant shape leaning on the upper deck's railing between circular cork lifebuoys painted in alternating red and white stripes. The 'Lady Northcote', about

a hundred yards away, bounced silently and swiftly on the waves
of an incoming tide. He watched the ship's foamy wake linger,
its eddies smashing against the dark grimy boulders below the
promontory's wall. He watched until the steamer became a dot,
vanishing at sea.

In the fortnight that followed he spoke little, neither to his
parents, his elder brother, or friends. He attended classes, came
home in time at three pm each day to catch the daily broadcast
of a short story on the BBC. He lived in the cinema, saw films
like Carol Reed's The Running Man, Mervyn LeRoy's Moment
To Moment, Henry King's Tender is the Night, Desire Me with
Robert Mitchum and Greer Garson, which strangely listed no
director in its credits. He read voraciously, sitting in bed with
the pillows propped up behind him like a convalescing patient.
Beside him at hand's reach was his bookcase made from raw
light wood crates found around the waterfront and brought home
with the help of a friend he rarely saw now. It stood against
the bedroom wall and to the left of its door, on the other side
of which was the drawing room. Now, some of the books he
had bought but never read, merely thumbed through, reading a
paragraph here and there, suddenly commanded his attention.
He absorbed Camus's The Myth of Sisyphus and The Rebel, was
fascinated by Kierkegaard's The Present Age; but most of all it
was Goethe's The Sorrows of Young Werther, which paralyzed
him after repeated contemplation. At the same time his initial
false indifference to Maba's leaving had crumbled, revealing the
perennial scaffold of his quiet desperation, which presided like a
lonely fortress from which he observed the pleasant contentment
of young lovers on the street, under the marquees of cinemas,
walking hand in hand along avenues leading to the seawall, or
side by side on their bicycles on their way to a fete. Even the
joviality of his parents: the rattling of ice in their glasses filled

with rum and ginger ale when entertaining friends, their laughter at cryptic comments he felt referred to him, the munching on fruit cake…all this seemed to him insensitive to what he had recently experienced. It was as if he and Maba had never existed, as proven by a law which recognized no possible normality, no benevolence outside its interpretive goal of protection for the 'innocent' as an anonymous class or specie, rather than specific individuals. It was not so much Maba's wrenching away that frustrated him to the level of a mental aberration now, but the feeling of being a victim of some traditional, or natural absurdity, which dawned on him as though it were just the beginning of what life had to offer.

Helped by the experience of reading Goethe's book, he concocted the idea that by removing his existence his presence for his family would return, all be it, painfully, which they deserved, he reasoned. He even laughed in sado-masochistic pleasure at an aphorism Camus had written, to the effect that the secret wish of every suicidal man is to witness his own funeral. In this fatalistic rationale he had not thought that Maba at least, wherever she was, preferred him alive rather than dead.

On one of those Georgetown evenings near the middle of the year, when after a searing day of sunshine and blue skies the atmosphere dims to a cool aura aided by an incoming tide at the city's doorstep, he felt brave enough—after much rumination while sitting on the edge of his bed before his bookcase with the colorful spines of paperback volumes which now appeared to have been his only true friends—to begin unscrewing the circular lid of a metal can which pumped a deadly DDT spray for the dispersal of mosquitoes at bedtime. He expected it would cause some pain upon imbibing, but would lead to a state of unconsciousness which would be the end of that! While unscrewing the top of the deadly container he heard the happy voices of his parents, the rattle of ice in their rum and coke drinks while entertaining a friend on the other side of his wall which defined the drawing room, and where the creak of his father's rocking chair was like the ticking of a time bomb in his hand.

As he raised the circular grooved metal mouth of the container to his lips he swore he heard his name being called. For a second he wondered if it was some schizoid voice within his own mind, but the second call of his name was clear enough to prove it was someone else's voice he now recognized. The eccentric hermit Oriental caretaker who lived in a crude little shack in the backyard of Maba's employers! What could this fool want at such a time! The deadly container was stuck in mid air before his lips, and he could smell its horrid chemical odor. When he heard his father's voice calling for him he realized he had to respond to the crazy hermit before one of his parents came into his bedroom to investigate what was delaying him, since his light was on and it was not his usual bedtime.

He screwed the foot long pump back unto the container, placed it under his bed, and rushed out to the drawing room, almost running across the polished floor to the open front windows which overlooked the gate and bridge. The caretaker hermit looked up at him and demanded in a loud belligerent voice a sum of money owed to him. He was about to yell back angrily that he had no idea what the hell he was speaking of, when the hermit under the cover of his previous loud tone of voice whispered that he had something for him, and pulled an envelope from his waist. He ran down the front stairs loudly exclaiming that he was coming to deal with this crazy accusation. At the gate the smiling dark Oriental man handed over a letter from Maba, who had used the hermit's name and address on an outer envelope which concealed another envelope addressed to him. Almost laughing he promised to buy the hermit a quarter bottle of rum for his loyalty, but the frail little man merely smiled and waved his offer aside, bidding him goodnight.

He walked back upstairs as calmly as possible and immediately locked himself within the washroom. He sat on the bowl and read Maba's fat careful handwriting, its blue ink from a fountain pen spelling out simple perfect English in lines across three pages torn out from a child's exercise book. But the best part of opening her envelope was the flowery fragrance which clung to a little blue bordered handkerchief folded in a triangle with her embroidered initials at one end which fell into his palm. He pressed the handkerchief to his nose repeatedly, and later when he stored it with her letter in an old battered brown suitcase under his bed, each time he opened the suitcase the scent and memory of the miraculous event once more flooded his room.

Language, words, he thought, after all the novels, stories, poems he had read, had never felt as precious as what he had read in her letter, which confirmed all the fantasies of love and longing he imagined they shared.

He returned to the company of his friends, jovial and gregarious. Drank beers, attended fetes and the city cinemas in groups again. But only a few friends whom he had told of Maba knew how close he had come to tragedy in the most casual manner. Since he had passed his exams in English, History, English Literature, French, Scripture, and Mathematics, he now held a certificate which entitled him to a job in the interior areas, in places similar to where Maba originated. One of his friends, a catholic like him, and certificated as well, knew of such openings at a catholic missionary school in Maba's region. He wasn't surprised when his father refused permission for him to fill one of the open positions, claiming, expectedly, that he was still in pursuit of "that girl". The truth however was, that was not his major intention, since Maba's letter had fulfilled and

wiped out most of his rebellion against their prohibited affair.
Her words had left him contented and resigned to their indefinite
banishment from each other. In his happiness he had thought
no further of any possible continuity to their affair, or possible
plan for it, which had been left unmentioned, perhaps even
for cautionary reasons, in her letter as well. When his friend
proposed applying for other positions in a school at the opposite
end of their country, almost on the border with Brazil, seven
hundred miles away from where Maba lived, and five hundred
miles away from the city, his father agreed to that.

They flew off in a Dakota over jungles with blossoming
yellow, red, and purple tree tops and the exposed red banks of
endless rivers meandering like gigantic anacondas below, until
the Dakota's wings began to dip and cant through the dry arid
mountain sides of valleys and they landed on the hot scalloped
white sand of a tribal village.

He spent six months in a Native Indian village at the top
of a low hill, invisible until you crossed a creek at its feet and
climbed its adjacent steep bank. The village was almost entirely
surrounded by the jagged blue peaks of a distant sierra, which
turned bright orange during each sunset. In off periods, he sat
shirtless on corrals and watched Native Indian vaqueros rope
then castrate bulls in order to fatten them, packing their empty
scrotums with salt before sewing them up with thin strips of
rawhide, then releasing the animals to buck with fury, kicking
up dust which watered his eyes in the glaring sun. Sometimes
he ventured into other native villages where there were antique
petroglyphs gouged into huge black circular rocks which cropped
up out of the savannah. Some of the rocks undulated across the
arid dusty terrain like a paleolithic shield, and huge soft plants
erupted here and there across their surface. He often lay in the
smooth soft flattened interior of these unknown green plants and

contemplated the jagged peaks of sierras on the horizon around him. Once he had an experience which left an indelible feeling of paradise within him. In a creek which lay at the bottom of a hill which concealed his village, he went down to bathe in the heat of the early afternoon, when most of the women of the tribe were out in the distant 'garden' fields, and the men lay in their hammocks waiting for evening to fall before their hunting trips began. In the creek he stumbled upon one of the most beautiful women (perhaps the most, it was said) in the village bathing alone. Feeling too awkward and self-conscious, he decided it would be prudish to turn back, though he certainly knew he would not enter the creek right then to bathe. She waved to him and continued bathing, as he sat on a rock overlooking the creek. He gazed anxiously at the surrounding scenery. She emerged nude, picked up a dress, which was all she had brought, and with it in her hands walked straight up hill towards him, saying: "Kaimen pownar, teacher!" with a smile as she went by. The phrase meant simply "Good day" in Wapisianna, her language. He watched her gleaming wet rust-red nude body with wide hips and firm buttocks below her long dripping black hair walk up hill in the searing sun against the clean blue sky, the soles of her bare feet coated with the hill's white sand.

So he was right about American Westerns being part of his culture, he thought, while splitting tree trunks for firewood at sunset, recalling with awe that scene in Shane when Alan Ladd began chopping at the root of a stubborn tree stump. Once, some young teenage Native Indian girls sat nearby on the lowered yoke of a cart silently observing him. When he noticed their smooth legs exposed by raised knees, and absence of their underwear, the axe almost missed its mark and found his shin instead. That experience had reminded him of what Maba had admitted of her first sexual experience with a neighbor, who had come over to her house when she was alone and deflowered her. He had not felt jealous of her neighbor, just relieved and encouraged that at least one of them was experienced in that area beyond mere reading.

On his return to the city he immediately noticed that his parents were stealing glances at him with some sort of sympathy, or reserved discretion. It was the hermit who told him that not long after he had left for the distant savannahs, Maba had run away to the city, joining other Native Indian girls who wanted independent lives outside the protection of those laws governing indigenous women. The hermit told him where she could be found at work, which was at a popular Oriental restaurant he knew well. When Maba first saw him she seemed overjoyed, yet her behavior was more impersonal, like a good friend, different from what he had known her to be, which seemed in-keeping with the fact that she had cut her long undulating waves of hair to a more practical and disguised style that now seemed to cast a demeanor of sacrificial necessity and determination on her face. Obviously an asset, he could see, in serving countless strange men, often friendly and flirtatious for unsaid reasons. A complete change from the sensitive and protective family atmosphere of his neighbor's household, where, for complicated legal reasons she was no longer welcome to serve.

Once they made an agreement that he would pick her up at the end of her day shift and take her home on the bar of his bicycle. What he had suspected was true. She was living deep within the city, in a section that long ago had been little laboring communities at the perimeter of small estates, which at the end of the 18th century colonial era had been left to deteriorate into ramshackle tenement yards with those of any race who survived mainly by unskilled labor. She had found a home, no doubt temporary, among Africans, Orientals, Portuguese, and mixed race individuals—even some native Indians like herself—who lived on low canting floors, muddy passage-ways laid with planks, public water pipes and galvanized washrooms at the edge of gutters choked with slimy refuse, while the nearby rutted street acted as a public forum for the continual fabrication of rumors, stories, arguments, often degenerating into violent fights, murders, which began as verbal abuse in colloquial speech influenced by, and adjusted to the uneducated patterns of the lifestyle it reflected.

He would later receive the linguistic brunt of this new environmental influence she had recently been weaned on, after the traumatic revelation from a close acquaintance (who upon leaving college had become a purser on the steamer plying the long route between the capital and Maba's remote district), that she matched the description of a girl who in payment for the steamer fare she did not possess, about five months or so ago, had slept in his cabin and berth. Of course he was staggered by this new information, which apparently was also possessed by his parents who seemed to beam with silent satisfaction at the confirmation of a fate they had predicted all along, and from which they excused themselves without any involvement as it played out. He resigned from his teaching post.

Between daily bouts of harsh cheap local rum which hastened intoxication and self-pity, he took to following Maba's movements clandestinely: hanging out at street corner shops, observing her with strange mature men much older than she was in different poor areas of the city. Until tracing her to the large third floor of a towering wooden building overlooking a large green canal left over from what had been an 18th century Dutch community near the riverside, he climbed the winding staircase to its veranda, and upon enquiring about her from one of the gaudily dressed and cosmetically made-up mestizo girls idling there, she appeared. Her red lip-stick lips, tight blouse, bright loose orange skirt and white high heels almost making him laugh out in masochistic inebriation. When she demanded how he had found her, and why he was here, to which he countered by asking if she knew a certain purser by a certain name from a certain ship, she released a torrent of expletives from the veranda overlooking the step he stood on, then raised her skirt revealing her legs, panties, and navel, shouting with apparent glee: "Dis is my cat, an I fuck wid who I like!" Indicating with an index finger the implied region of their dispute. He staggered down the stairs silently, picked up his bicycle and rode away, determined never to follow or speak to her again.

Of course the news of her vagabond return to the city in his absence had added to his already nagging guilt that he had aided the resulting messiness of the whole affair. He withdrew into himself again, but this time it brought a certain amount of pleasure, as though he had aged wisely, or matured in a leap. He didn't want to share this feeling with his seventeen year-old peers, since they were involved in more respectable intrigues with city girls who had none of the experiences of Maba. It was a pleasure to sit in his favorite city cinemas like Plaza, Globe, Metropole, or Empire around the corner in his neighborhood at 4.30 pm matinees almost every other day, enjoying the relevant self-pitiful lyrics and melodies of Pop songs like : "I'm Just a Lonely Boy," "Dream Lover," "Cathy's Clown," "Crying in the Rain," "Downtown," "It Tears Me Up," or instrumentals like: "Love is Blue," "Theme From a Summer Place," "The Girl From Ipanema" while waiting on films like: Walk on the Wild Side; The Sun Also Rises; The Last Time I Saw Paris; Butterfield 8; Go Naked in the World, to begin.

And then out of the blue a letter addressed to him arrived from Maba's district. It was from an old friend who had been his senior in college and was now a mathematics teacher in the higher forms of a Roman Catholic missionary school about four miles away from Maba's hilltop community. They needed an English teacher for the entire school, since no other teacher possessed a certificate in this subject always found difficult to master at certified exams. It was one of the subjects he had passed with flying colors, and the mathematics teacher had heard and recommended him to his headmistress, a local Nun of Portuguese descent, who promptly sent for him.

The letter created a flare up of memories about the barefoot white man gone Native who had frequented his house after long absences in the wilderness. And yet meeting Maba had never really provoked a desire to live in her region as much as the memory of the old adventurer did now. Maba could have his city, he would have her distant hills, he decided. His parents didn't object to his departure this time for a post in Maba's district, since it was no secret to them that she was now in the city, and the circumstances of her presence there made her sudden return home unlikely.

He found himself on the same steamer, standing at the same starboard rail between the same circular life buoys, staring at the same long stone jetty parallel to the river's mouth where he had stood looking at Maba, who had stood looking back at him from where he was standing now. He saw the entire coast slowly vanish as the ship cut a path of foam straight out into the Atlantic, until its water changed from opaque ochre to transparent dark green in a sudden and perfect straight line. The shape of the coast, invisible from the Demerara river's mouth beside the city, made a steep north-westerly turn for a few hundred miles, passing another river's mouth at least twenty-one miles wide, and two others of lesser sizes, until it reached a peninsula adjacent to the mouth of the nearby Orinoco river.

He saw the ship's wake unfurling in lines of white foam under the lights of the stern as night fell. Saw the stars low above the surface of the sea when the bow dipped then rose in deep craters of waves ripping strips of foam skyward as he stumbled across the upper deck among silent Native Indians huddled in deck chairs around the inner cabins reserved for commuting merchants. He dipped beneath hammocks slung within the lower deck, where the odor of fried fish and eggs from the bright galley tingled the nausea of sea-sickness, forcing him to retreat to the frontal deck beside gold-toothed mulatto sailors in their thick demin tunics sitting around the rim of the hold covered in a tarpaulin reeking of diesel and cargo, sparks from their cigarettes fluttering briefly like shooting stars in the cool, stiff, steady current of sea breeze.

Back in his deck chair he went over the events that had brought him to where he was now, and fell in and out of sleep to the rhythmic rolling of the ship and steady drone of its turbines. When some sailors wound up the green tarpaulins that had prevented squalls from drenching passengers, he saw it was dawn and they were parallel to a long distant white beach lined with palm trees. It was like another planet, completely desolate, deserted, as if being discovered for the first time by humans. The surface of the sea had become hard little ripples, grey with mud in a falling tide as they approached an opening in the low lying swampy terrain. Palm trees grew out of dark water glittering in the first rays of morning sun. The trees that dominated the stark still terrain of rotting green and purple vegetation, mossy tree trunks and branches, were half submerged, reflecting their wobbling shapes among species of birds unknown to him feeding on fishes, insects, and baby reptiles in the slowly rippling unearthly water. The ship's railings trembled above the hard current as it entered the passage, and pink flamingoes flew lazily over the hold, some landing on the sharp tip of the white bow cutting the thick muddy current below, and on the upper deck's railings beaded with cold dew from mist clouding the top of the flanking vegetation.

It was an obscure terrain where 16th and 17th century Portuguese, Spanish and Anglo Elizabethan conquistadores had ventured, roaming rivers that were nameless to them, pursuing the mirage of a City of Gold that had been hatched and embellished in delirious, feverish stories and adventures affected by untamed nature and hallucigenic cuisine. A watery landscape where nothing was naturally permanent, where once had been sea was now land, and where once had been land was now sea; where confused maps were drawn and redrawn according to competing European nations, projecting mostly the wishes of men and their empires rather than the wishes of planetary nature.

The ship's horn blasted before it rounded a bend where the passage met a wide river. A settlement appeared, and the arrival of the ship was like a celebration for the polyglot crowd that greeted it on the long high sturdy wharf made of massive planks from the famous water-resistant greenheart trees.

The settlement behind the wharf which he saw from the height of the ship's deck was once a boomtown during a gold rush at the beginning of the 20th century. Now it was almost a ghost town. There were a few shops leading from the wharf to the remains of a street parallel to the river, where a handful of derelict houses and a church canted into the soil sprouting tall weeds, palm and coconut trees. The signs of other streets remained, overgrown with the jungle, and vine-clogged skeletons of buildings that must have been saloons, hotels, brothels, merchants' stores and gold dealers' offices were left like evidence of when the town bustled and brawled with rum drinking, whoring, and commerce brought by all sorts of people who arrived from the capital and three hundred miles of coastland, as well as neighboring Venezuela.

Standing on the wharf were a few dozen people, barefoot
Native Indian men and women, the latter in incandescent yellow,
pink, blue nylon and satin dresses, holding babies against their
hips, fat Oriental merchants in felt hats, lean black men in collar
and tie, attached to the Ministry of Transport no doubt, a few
uniformed black policemen, as well as a few Venezuelan mestizo
men in straw hats and wrinkled water-washed white cotton suits,
owners of the launches moored at the side of the wharf's tall
structure with wooden steps going down into the lapping water.

Outstanding in this crowd was his friend, the teacher, dressed
like no one else in his vertical blue, white, and pink striped Bossa
Nova shirt with its wide jersey collar and buttoned at the sides
of his waist. He wore glove tight white jeans, and dirty white
canvas espadrilles. His tall black body had broad shoulders, and
his flat-top hairstyle made him look like Cannonball Adderly on
one of their favorite Jazz album covers. Even here, he thought,
the teacher looked no different from when they had feted in the
city, hung out on stools on cool late afternoons around the bar
of the Blue Light Café on Camp Street, bright kerchiefs tied
around their necks, sports shirts open down their chests, sipping
milkshakes, their elbows leaning on the bar made of special
smooth thick silver zinc sheets, while listening to the Café's
instrumentals by Booker T & The MGs, The Shadows, The
Ventures, Hugh Masakela, Dave Brubeck, Charlie Parker, Miles
Davis, Stan Getz, Antonio Carlos Jobim, Sergio Mendes, etc.

The teacher stood waiting on his arrival while tapping a wild
school cane against the side of his leg. He bounded down the
gangplank in woven jute bag espadrilles, holding his suitcase which
kept the fragrance of Maba's initialed triangular-folded hankie,
feeling sticky and tired, his creased white shirt and blue Buffalo
jeans smelling of the ship's diesel and musty canvas deck chair.

"Waiting on your Mail Order bride I see, just like Heston in

The Naked Jungle, right?" he said, pointing and laughing at the teacher's wild cane and apparent deliberate cinematic pose.

"Glad you made it Reds." Reds had been his false name by the teacher, who added: "This is Jerry, you're going to need him for a while," indicating a young white creole man from the region who eagerly took his suitcase as they walked to the edge of the wharf and descended its greenheart steps to the level of the dark river where a weather-beaten blue launch bounced, filling up with passengers who had arrived on the same steamer.

It was here, during the crossing to the other side of the river towards an abrupt gap in the jungle indicating the beginning and end of a road with a few parked Land Rovers, that an eclipse occurred in his relation to the two banks. He had no idea where was north, south, east or west. The wharf with the moored steamer, and the gap at a diagonal in the jungle on the other side of the river, seemed interchangeable, like a concave/convex illusion, which continued at the windows of the launch, where passengers sat, their weight bringing the vessel down almost to the level of the massive silent river, whose smooth surface, dark like Pepperpot, but with a rust-red transparency, swayed, and was littered with large floating dead insects he had never seen before, dust like a thin skin, and islands of curled green lianas; all swaying and drifting lazily almost at the level of his head, eyes, and neck above the frighteningly close surface of the water.

They sat at the back of an open Land Rover which sped along the straight asphalt but decaying and pot-holed road that began across the river, cutting through the dry parched stillness of the palm laden landscape. Lone little Native Indian peasant men in broad sweat-stained felt hats and khaki clothes bent at wide intervals with gleaming machetes, clearing the wild vegetation forever creeping onto the lonely road sides. Occasionally off the road-sides, a hut, or rather a shelter appeared—little more than nailed together boards grey and weather-beaten—with a rusted zinc roof. The faces of Native Indian women would appear in gaps between boards of these shelters, and sometimes the unmistakable mixed features of the African and Native Indian, with the even more enigmatic features of a child held at the hip, as the jeep flashed by. After a good many miles they climbed to the top of a hill where the jungle gave way to further distant rolling vistas of hills with spongy green vegetation, and clouds like the shapes of various animals migrating eternally across the bleached blue sky. Sumptuous sprawling farms appeared, the land well tilled, acres of fruit trees, and at least one large general store with a local Anglo-Chinese name. An entire community emerged spaced along the hill-top where the road, well paved now, was lined with massive white Eucalyptus trees, their white paper bark flaking, flapping, and verdant heads roaring in a soothing brisk breeze. Rubber trees stood elegantly beside lawns with a Guest House, a small hospital, Police Station, District Commissioner's house, large vats for rain water, even a lawn tennis court.

He knew this was the community of Maba, but could only imagine her house somewhere within the surrounding forest. They sped downhill and left the community behind, passed a branch road which led to a riverside community of shops beside the wharf of another river, umber-colored, a deep winding tributary of the one with the first settlement the steamer had been left at. They sped over humped wooden bridges whose loose boards rattled under the jeep's wheels and above black creeks overhung with flowering vegetation, climbed another towering hill along a winding road with terraced earthen steps leading to Native Indian houses on the hilltop, and up there where the road curved, offering vistas of flowing jungle-clad hills to the horizon of stagnant white clouds tinged with grey precipitation, he caught a glimpse of the umber river following them like a smooth arc cut out of the flat surrounding jungle carpet where the wharf on the tributary stood. Later, in his job as a teacher, he took walks to that panoramic hilltop spot, and would often stand and gaze at the stunning contrast of the distant weekly steamer's moored white bow, its red, black, and white funnel and white lifeboats above the dark river, on its second stop, cut out briefly in the pristine green expanse to the horizon. Then he would walk back to his house with its veranda overlooking the same river from another viewpoint, below the sloping green hillside where an Agricultural Station had become his home for the duration of his sojourn as the community school's English teacher.

On his first return to the capital during school holidays, he caught the steamer from its second terminus and travelled back to the ex-boomtown at its first terminus. Standing at its upper deck rail, watching the river's black water cut by the bow into curling white-lipped waves, the fresh scent of the close, tall jungle's chlorophyll in the pristine breeze tingled his nostrils. When in the midday sun the steamer docked at the decaying settlement of the old boomtown, he bounded down the gangway, walked through the wharf's huge bond with its galvanized roof and noisy laborers, and along the short rutted dirt road to a deserted small dilapidated blue shop that called itself a Beer Garden.

There was one Native Indian girl, probably about sixteen or seventeen, behind the wooden counter, and when he saw her face his heart skipped a beat because of her resemblance to Maba. He found it difficult to take his eyes off her short thick body which glowed with a smooth oily sienna color in the humid sunshine against a pink close-fitting satin dress halfway up her thighs and clinging to her belly's slope.

"What you want?" she said, "Why you staring at me like that?"

"You remind me of someone I once knew, that's all."

"You loved her nuh? And she do you wrong. Drink a beer and tell me your story. What she name?"

He was laughing when he told her "Maba", tickled by the sight of this girl he thought of as probably left- over evidence of the settlement's legendary ribald days. "Give me a Banks beer," he said.

"So she had my name too? I name Maba too," she said, backing him, opening the big rusty freezer that operated by kerosene, since there was no electricity in the run-down port. She turned back to him smiling with nice even short teeth in a thin lipped mouth, just like Maba's, but her hair wasn't wavy, just jet black, long and glossy to her shoulders. She uncapped his beer, staring at him, not the money he put on the counter.

"You like me too. I could see it. I like you too," she added.

"You just met me and you like me? You're pulling my leg."

"Why not? How long Maba take to like you, and you to like she?"

It was a question that caught him off guard, and in honesty he would have had to admit, instantly, in retrospect. He began drinking his beer.

"I know she hurt you," the girl continued, staring at him, "but I not like that, I like Kaywana, I'm an old-time buck girl."

"Kaywana!" he said in a startled voice, "You've read Edgar Mittelholzer's Children of Kaywana?"

"All three books. Is not three books? I could read and write you know, I'm not no stupid buck girl. Look," she said, stretching her bare arms across the counter, "hold my arm." Her dress was sleeveless, her arms sturdy, smooth, and hot. "I'm not going to say loose my arm, like Kaywana tell August Vyfuis the first time he hold she arm."

He drank from the bottle. The beer was cold enough. He wasn't sure he wasn't dreaming.

"Suppose I say I must have you now, right now, today, just like August Vyfuis told Kaywana?" He said, sure that would put an end to her play-acting.

"Ok, we could do something quick, I know your boat waiting," she said, moving from the counter to one of the shutters at the side of the shop with a view to a bushy small trench. She pulled in the shutter quietly. He stared at her legs that were exposed up to the beginning of her wide buttocks as she bent over some cartons and pulled in the shutters of a few more windows. Just then the steamer blew; its first warning that it would un-moor shortly. She ran around the counter to the front of the shop as he stood up from one of the rickety stools. "Feel me" she said, and quickly slid the sides of her dress up to her tight yellow nylon underwear. He put down his beer and embraced her, their arms around each-other and pelvises grazing. The shop's door was half-closed beside them, and a sharp vertical line of sunlight fell across the dirt floor and rough wooden counter, dissecting the dark coolness of the interior. The ship blew again, and she said: "Ok, go, but don't forget this Maba! Take your beer!"

He ran out the door with the bottle of Banks beer in his hand, his Buffalo jeans still bulging with half his erection. He looked back laughing at her face, also laughing, leaning out the shop door. He ran to the edge of the wharf where the ship was already about three feet away, jumping the gap of swirling dark water with banana and avocado and citrus orange skins stirred up below starboard, landing on the deck to the applause and jokes of sailors and the purser who had kept his suitcase.

When he returned from two-weeks of holidays in the city he

walked down the same dirt road to the Beer Garden, but found it closed, perhaps permanently. When he did see Maba again it was fleeting, from a distance. Once she was sitting at the back of a jeep roaring by on a long straight jungle road between hills; another time on a launch heading somewhere down river. Though she must have recognized him, neither of them waved. Then one day when he decided to walk back from the second steamer terminus to the hill community where he taught, four miles away, he found himself approaching a lone girl at the side of the long deserted road between distant hills. As he neared the smiling figure he knew it was Maba. She wore a flowing blue and white striped dress which ended just above her knees, a few exercise and text books were in her hand, and she carried a shoulder bag. She looked the same, though less sensually dressed.

"I know we would meet again," she said smiling, and held out her hand. He held it, feeling its heat and slight perspiration in the stark sun directly overhead. The edges of the jungle beside them were alive with whistles, screeches, squawks, and invisible skirmishes. She stood at the edge of the road, about a dozen yards away from a dark creek that flowed into the jungle from beneath a humped wooden bridge.

"You look like you were waiting for me," he said, deciding to encourage the kind of dialogue she seemed to like.

"If is so, is because you tell me to!" she said, laughing.

"But we never met again since that time in the shop," he said.

"So?" she said, "Didn't I tell you don't forget me?"

"Right," he said, "I remembered to remember without remembering, that's why we met again," he said, laughing.

"You're talking wild, I like men who talk wild," she said, quoting a part of Kaywana's dialogue with August Vyfuis.

They were holding onto each other's hands. He pulled her to him. He could smell her light sweat mixed with faint sweet soap. Her face was inches away, looking up at his. She put her hands around his neck and said: "I wish you could take me in the jungle now and do what you want wid me, but this place all swampy, there's nowhere to lie down."

"I know," he said, "but what are you doing here?"

"I'm waiting on my father to come and take me home, to a hill up the creek. Look," she said, "he coming now." He saw a Native Indian man in white shirt and short khaki pants, a broad straw hat on his head, paddling a low bark canoe on the creek's black swirling water. They held unto each other even as they slowly began to move apart. Their outstretched hands were the only part of their bodies touching as they stared at each other silently.

They let go, and he watched her walk through wild grass brushing her calves before stepping into the canoe, which had reversed, so that her father backed him while she faced her father when she stooped then sat, placing her books at her feet, her dress covering her knees, her face smiling as the canoe slid over the black water littered with tiny yellow leaves from the canopy overhead, until it vanished.

He continued walking along the totally deserted and simmering hot straight road filled with diverse sounds from the tall parallel jungle.

AMANTE CARAQUENO

Siesta begins with the roar of brightly painted metallic shop doors being lowered. Caracas looks like a metropolis of multi-colored skyscrapers in a futuristic Science Fiction film, but if we saw most of the calendar pages in the city they would be set at May 1986. The city's white terraces and pastel-colored architectural mazes winding through a green sunlit valley are seen from a bus, one of many jostling each other down the steep incline of hectic Avenida Urdaneta, before it becomes Avenida Andres Bello, on a congested urban rim offering brief panoramic views of other parts of the urban valley down below.

Down there, at the beginning of Siesta, over the heads of short bristling palm trees on Avenida Las Palmas, and both sides of El Rosal with its traffic- jammed cars at stop-lights and cross-walks, is the tall elongated triangular La Previsora building with its digital clock in glowing block numbers shining through the smog of steamy days. The long cafes under canvas awnings are beginning to fill up with caballeros arriving in their white and cream Pierre Cardin linen suits. Their little leather Tote bags tucked under their arms, their El Universal newspapers or Imagen Arts magazines open on round cafe tables while they order bacon and omelette sandwiches, Arepas with sausage, chicken, beef, or just grated cheese, hamburgers and café con leches.

That is after they have sipped their liqueurs with female companions who have arrived hurriedly, late as usual, chattering away in melodious Caraqueno accents aided by frenetic little hand gesticulations as though they were brushing away flies (and sometimes they are), or offering some invisible object to each-other in their upturned palms. They will usually settle for a French omelette with French toast, or a Spaghetti Carbonera; the plumper ones a Pabellon Criollo, with its shredded beef in marinated spiced tomatoes, black beans and a few slices of ripe plantain on the side. After, Belmont Suaves lit quickly by expensive gold lighters, leave a nice drying taste of tobacco (the shamanistic ritual of a preserved legacy of Native Culture?) on the tongue, a taste further blended with sips from their little glasses of Cointreau or Grand Mariner, which have just been laid before them by the moustached waiter in his black bowtie, white shirt, and black trousers, who afterwards spins his oval cork-lined tray over their heads and swiftly walks away.

The 8 and 9 am morning mood of cool mist floating down the rim of the Avila mountains on the left side of Caracas, has evaporated in bright sunlight and the scalding vapor of endless traffic-jammed Toyota Jeeps, Mercedes Benz, Renaults and Volkswagons. The beautiful elegant office girls, many of only guessed at exact racial origin, in their almost transparent long cotton skirts and slim high heels tapping the pave, have long vanished with fresh bouquets of flowers for the boutiques, banks, and high rise offices on Sabana Grande, Calle Las Delicias, Calle Negrino, Avenida Casanova, Chaicaito and Bello Monte. The zinc counters in the cafes littered with silver Bolivars are swept up from time to time, and the garbage pails filled with little plastic cups discarded with a nonchalant reflex after their café con leches and morons have been sipped or gulped by moustached men in tapered trousers and matching short jackets, briefcases or Tote bags under their arms, various fragrances wafting off some of their necks and well brushed varieties of hair.

The offices and stores are now closed for Siesta, but the porno cinemas, bars and cafes are open for those office workers flooding the sidewalks, where also a number of flamboyant artists with uncut hair, beards, white slacks, colored espadrilles, and tight shirts with button down pockets, are idle in little groups of two or three, smoking little cigars and talking extravagantly while glancing around, trying to identify people they know; office girls in particular: striding up, walking beside them, touching their elbows suggestively with bright smiles and a loud "Hola!," as though they are the best of friends, their one-sided comments repeatedly filled with the word "cuadro," followed by "Mi amor," and "cheveri,"and "muy lindo", and "cafecita," and "cervesa," and finally "Caras," and "Ciao," as they are brushed off with weary smiles.

Through little square perforations in a bright blue wall over-looking a winding white marble stairway leading to three spacious floors in a three-storied building, can be seen a shut polished door to one of the hotel rooms that line the hallway running along a corridor on the third floor at the top of the stairs. There are two little hallways around the two corners of two parallel walls on each side of the ample stairway, but these hallways are invisible from the stairs whose entire outer wall is covered in chessboard perforations. Looking back through these perforations the sidewalk with its siesta strollers, the artists, the packed outdoor cafes, bars, restaurants, porno cinemas, and so on, can be seen.

Behind one of the closed doors of a room on the third floor we see a young colored man with an orange towel wrapped around the middle of his no doubt nude body. He is reclining on one of two beds reading a coffee table art book on the 18th century libertine French painter Fragonard from the French Riviera town of Grasse, famous for its perfume. On the cover of the book is a reproduction of that perhaps well known Fragonard painting of a girl in a swing, while stooping in the garden around her and gazing up her exposed legs, is a young cavalier. Opposite the young man's bed we see a small wooden desk upon which a notebook is open at adjacent blank pages with an unopened fountain pen between them. Outside the room, the Avila mountain range above the Caracas valley projects shadows and giant waves of sunlight appearing and disappearing against the single dusty pink-tinted window pane on the left side of his room.

Across the hall, about five yards opposite his closed door, a girl whose sounds he had grown familiar with over his two weeks of an indefinite stay, hummed a tune in the city's buzz. He had grown accustomed to her mysterious presence, not knowing anything about her, whether she worked—which seemed unlikely since she was at home all morning, or at anytime, without a pattern—or maybe she was vacationing, or…..He had given up guessing about her, and began to enjoy her close presence and attractive feminine habits.

He got up and opened his door, leaving it ajar. In his mind his reason was he wanted some extra air flowing over the Avila range, filtering through the perforations in the wall overlooking the stairway; but also knowing that she kept her door open frequently, meant he would glimpse her passing across the oblong space of her room's visible interior. Indeed the location of his bed and his position on it allowed such a view when he looked away from the book in his hands. Each time her rubber slippers slapped her shifting heels he felt compelled to look her way, and he often saw her eyes meet his between their open doors.

Once he had come down to the lobby when he had first arrived, and met her dancing to her Walkman in the hotel lobby.

"Quien usted? Como se llama?" She had said, unplugging her ears and squinting vaguely in distrust at him it seemed, her left hand held out, palm upward towards him. He had told her in simple Spanish his name, and that he was from a neighboring country, the only one on the continent whose national language was English. "Ahhh!" she had exclaimed, as though someone had suddenly stabbed her, her eyes opening wide with surprise as though he had admitted a guarded secret, a crime, or indicated a precious location. She had lapsed into immediate silence while staring at him intensely, as though having come face to face with an alien from another planet.

In any case he had to run, and said so, slipping past her, out between two rows of potted plants at the hotel's entrance and towards the curb where Avenida Casanova sloped down beside commuters waiting on 'Por Puesto' buses, since it was after five in the afternoon when he usually went down Casanova, past the little side streets with art stores, boutiques, Lebanese cafes; past Calle Collegio; a big hotel across the street; an Argentine parilla restaurant denoted by its popular Constructivist neon sculpture outside; and a colossal new mall being built. At a little square beside a store of modern furniture designs, he socialized with a Caraqueno bohemian painter who resembled one of those pioneer characters (only darker) with a huge moustache, lifting a large cornocopia in Tiepolo's mural America. He never felt like an alien there, among all sorts of foreigners in love with Caracas like himself: A young Spanish architect from Barcelona who recited lines to him in French from Saint-John Perse's long poem Anabasis: "Terre arable du songe, qui parle de batir…", and was thrilled when he continued the stanza with: "Jai vu la terre distribute en de vastes espaces et ma pensee n'est point distraite du navigateur."

They had become eager colleagues meeting at the little square most evenings. There was also the Swiss girl, in her blue jeans, white cotton shirt and sandals, her uncombed blonde hair turning reddish bronze over her tanned flushed face in the valley's hard sunshine. She was dreamy, interested in nothing urgent, in love with the streets, the cafes where they sat down to Lebanese Shawarmas and cold Tamarind juice, watching the crowds as evening arrived casting a transparent pink/magenta hue across the white walls of nearby buildings and white table cloths before them, as song after song by Jose Luis Rodriguez, Caridad Canelon, Carina, Ilan Chester and others could be heard sharing the same Caracas FM band. Among them could often be seen two tall Italian drifters from Milan, their hairy chests exposed under tight sports shirts; one blond, the other black-haired, both handsome by any standard, their well-cut trousers and suede boots revealing a life in fashion perhaps, but here just content to sit beside the sidewalk and contemplate the sky, feeling the twilight coolness of the Avila breeze, sometimes watching the painter of the square, their mutual friend, at work, as they opened a bottle of Campari, sharing out plastic cups stuffed with ice from a large plastic bag the painter would order one of his assistants to find in a jiffy, appreciating how Coca-Cola foamed and bubbled over their Campari as everyone relaxed further, their conversations shifting from Spanish to Italian to English to French.

And then one siesta there she was, standing with a smile just outside his door which was ajar, with that Penelope Cruz body and Selma Hayak face, as though she were screen-testing for some role. Silently, as though expecting her, he had stood up and opened the door completely before rushing back to the open Fragonard art book on his bed. She had walked in slowly. He understood her rapid words mentioned her name as Silvana, then spoke about the heat while he glanced at her body outlined in the thin sheet of a silver night gown. They were the same, she said clearly in Spanish with a smile, glancing at the towel he wore around him. Then she sat on the edge of his bed gazing ahead. "Do you know Fragonard?" he said in Spanish, her head of smooth black hair bent, almost touching his of kinky strands, as she whispered,

"Muy lindo!" looking at a reproduced painting on the open page depicting a scene where two lovers embraced yearningly at the center of a bedroom floor, the male stretching back to bolt the unlocked door. "Muy lindo!" she cried again, staring at each painting of this libertine from terraced Grasse who passed away from a heart attack while eating ice cream, he told her in Spanish. "Mentira!" she said, laughing, and he replied: "Porque no?" getting up, saying he should take a shower, which made her ask if she should leave. He said no, it was Ok, and she stood up, swaying to his clothes in the open closet, her small hands gliding over Yves Saint Laurent, Armani, Emmanuel Ungaro, Daniel Hetcher, her voice whispering: "Muy lindo!" repeatedly.

In the shower he was not sure, but seemed to hear his leather Tote bag unclick, then re-lock; a sound too familiar for the shower's hiss to erase. Her slender curves turned, x-rayed through her gown, facing him, when he emerged from the bathroom dressed, eyeing his Tote bag with distrust. New as the look on her face (was it proud or scared?) came her voice, which did not stall as it invited him across the hall to her room. And she was gone, leaving behind nothing but the fading hint of sweet soap in her wake, while he followed in a sleep-walking state.

Dumbfounded, surprised, stepping no further than her door he giggled at the clutter—the bikinis, the lingerie, skirts, blouses, bright cotton slacks, overflowing her bed, tumbling unto the floor. "Tu bienvenido algo tiempo," she said, adding, "Mi amor," while dusting this, fixing that, rapid as a hare, as though no one but herself was there. So accepting, he withdrew, his "Ok," like silence, like nothing more to do except cross the hallway a half-dozen steps back to his door.

And it was true, half his Bolivars were missing when he checked his Tote bag. Not much, but sufficient to keep him interested in her, at least negatively. What would she say?

Search me? Search my room? These were the only scenes he could imagine, lying back in bed, curious about her life.

That night, dressed in some of the clothes she had inspected in his closet and liked, fragranced by 'Krizia Uomo', and seated on a black leather sofa facing the door to the lobby, he wondered what more she might have in store for him. Outside, beyond the potted plants beneath the blue and white striped canvas entrance canopy, he could see the El Rosal district's increasing traffic and hear the hum and honks from nearby Avenida Casanova which sloped down to a traffic jammed crawl.

From about midnight to dawn he intended to play once more among those friends he knew would suddenly appear, well dressed, excited, spirits already lifted by glasses of Tanqueray, or a few Cardinals,—which because of its pure spring water was the potent beer of their choice—talking rapidly, almost dancing on their feet at the clean corner of Casanova and Negrino, as golden kinetic bars of light climbed higher and higher above them, becoming a glass of sparkling golden Polar beer filling up on the roof of a nearby skyscraper against the mauve sky, it's up and down reflection flashing on and off the bonnets of parked cars. Other kinetic designs in the distance appeared in a flash out of the dark, then bit by bit vanished; then appeared again on various levels of the hills of nearby Bello Monte. The hands of his friends pressed to their chests then to his in split second gesticulations accompanied by phrases like : "Mira chico," "Benga conmigo," "Toma un othro cervesa, no?" " Si, cheveri, hombre," "Escuche, benga ahorita por una nota, rapido," "Yo tengo plata," etc. Sometimes equally suave vendors would appear with little folded paper towels wet and cool with cologne, patting their necks and chests, wiping away the city's film of smog from their faces. Cigarettes from red packs of 'Astor' or blue and white 'Belmont Suave' would then be shaken out and lit with matches, perhaps because it felt more manly to cup a lit match like the huge Malboro cowboy painted on the side of a nearby skyscraper. Everyone would be undecided whether to continue down Avenida Casanova to a window table inside Hotel Coliseo, or rub shoulders in tight little Tio Pepe on Calle Negrino, or maybe just stroll down that side street, turn left on Sabana Grande, then stop for hamburgers and merengadas under the orange plexiglass arced tops of Café Memphis; or perhaps walk a little further down Sabana Grande to Cafe La Vesuviana on Collegio where the rich intellectual girls, some just back from studying at the Sorbonne, their Toyota jeeps parked across the street from La Vesuviana, might be in a generous mood, sending a bottle of liqueur, or one of Vesuviana's hot Pizzas over to their table in memory of some brief affair with one of the bohemian artists among them.

And then someone might turn up the heat, and off to cozy Bar Milano on Calle Las Delicias they would go, or even the romantic tables and sexy floor show further down the street at Moulin Rouge might become appropriate. Here the atmosphere might lead to one or two couples forming, and they would end up strolling along crowded Sabana Grande at midnight, window shopping, peeking in at Steele's bookstore at the end of the street to see what new titles were laid out on the tables; then crossing the square with that tall outdoor kinetic Jesus Soto sculpture of suspended yellow iron rods chiming in the breeze at Centro Commercio Chacaito; and if they went down the stairs to Clara de Sujo's lower level patio art gallery they might be lucky to see a genuine Braque cubist collage, a Miro or Tapies canvas on an easel, or an Alexander Calder mobile through its glass pane, before coming up again and hurrying down to La Jungla at the end of an open corridor, past bookstores, art stores, and boutiques, and prior to even ordering drinks head right out onto the dance floor surrounded by the painted patterns of wild tropical animal skins on the club's black walls flashing under multi-colored lights, as Baltimora sang "Tarzan Boy".

⁜⁜⁜⁜⁜⁜

Now, without proof, he knew it was Silvana's heels he heard tapping down the marble staircase. Looking to his left he saw her come into view, then stop before turning on one tall thin heel, its upraised sole and tip as though pointing his way. His eyes slid by her golden toe-nails exposed above the high heel's lotus-tipped sole, leapt beyond yellow straps criss-crossing her slender tanned instep, and rose along her glove-tight pants. Black satin, he thought, watching how it clung to her thighs, swung around one wide round corner of her hip, pinching her narrow waist. "Senor," she said, even though she knew his name, looking down interrogatingly at him, her little red lips in a mild smile, and moist black hair sleekly combed to one side like the wing of a bird. "Senor," she said again in a childish melodious tone, "tu tenga una cita?" And he could have lied and said no, he had no appointment, nowhere to go, because he was suddenly captivated by some other choice. But he didn't reply, just watched how her tanned bronze belly gleamed when her yellow top was raised slightly by her little hand with a few thin silver rings as she walked by him on the lobby floor, then turned, like a model on a runway, and walked back to him a little faster, with a pronounced pounce of slight twists and turns, her tanned right hand gently rubbing her naked belly and exposed navel as she stopped before him and said in a giggling tone: "Entonces, si tu no tengo algo cita, me quiero hamburguesa con papas fritas!"

And with that brazen request for hamburger and French fries he exploded: "Donde esta mi plata Flaca?" But perhaps his words referring to her as a thieving bitch were exactly what she wanted to hear; she stood still and silent, one hand on her cocked hip, as though digesting his knowledge of her theft. It was her friend, an Afro-Caraqueno local beauty behind the lobby counter who answered him: "Cretino!" she shouted, "Tu no comprendo nada!" Frowning at him then turning to answer the ringing phone.

What could he say? Did he discard something with his accusation? Yet Silvana who uttered nothing in return, approached him calmly now, her swaying figure, he thought, defining the terms of some agreement she, or both of them, he and her, had concocted in her mind?

Calmly she stood before him, then bent one knee in shiny fabric on the sofa's edge in the space between his legs, opening her small leather purse, silently leaning forward as though he didn't exist, peering into some visionary future contained in the mirror behind his head. Like someone touching up her reflection she primped her face delicately in the tall and wide mirror. He could see nothing else before him but the way her skin-tight satin pants folded smoothly into a small imprinted triangle below her slightly sloping belly.

Beginning to sweat he slid out of the trap she set above his lap, darting for the stairs, his door, his latch. Places and things that in comparison to her felt painlessly innocent. Running up the stairway he heard the lobby clerk's voice pleading theatrically with him from below: "No no Senor! Por favor, no junquito!" That obscure last word, the name of a local vicinity apparently, he had learnt also meant masturbation. The laughter of the two girls echoed in the space below the staircase before he vanished behind his slamming door.

There was that bed again, and upon it the monograph on Fragonard open at another seduction scene. Flipping back its pages, there again was that picture she liked, like a scene ready for her knock, so soft when it came, a few minutes later. Her face, his face, his hands, her hands, her waist bent back, her hand, like the man's in the reproduced painting exposed on his bed, outstretched latching his door after she came in swiftly. His kiss on her warm neck, her eyes, the bedside lamp, its glow upon her bronze-gold legs revealed when her satin pants lay like a whirlpool on the floor, as outside, nighttime Caracas roared.

Inside, his voice asked her to walk again, back and forth, as she had done before in the lobby. This time, before him, her shining band of silver silk slid down, revealing where her flesh was lighter, protected from the beach, the sun, she said, since she took the teleferico cable car up over the Avila mountain range, out of Caracas, and down to the beach on the other side of the city almost daily, when not modeling, or attending classes in sociology. There was nothing more to tell, she said, except that her father owned the hotel.

Then her slender opening thighs, her pursed lips, her hips flashing back and forth, left and right between his palms pressed down on either side of her slim curvaceous body. Meanwhile, Caracas rippled in blazing kinetic signs above and below, as all the meregadas and batidos he had consumed at soda fountains over the past two weeks began to shoot out of him.

Then there he was, at the little desk, bent over his pen, writing another word, another line, as she, stooping beside him, massaged his leg, saying: "Otra vez, mi amor."

RERUN

Now that she had some good leads, now that she knew which clubs in Toronto he frequented, she caught a flight there after the New York party for her latest film. During the party she had deliberately chummed up to a young Canadian actor in the cast who plays some whizz kid on computers—a role fast becoming a new Hollywood staple for no other reason, she thought, than the producer's eye on the contemporary youth market. The Canadian, despite his amazing ability to appear unflinchingly serious and masculine in every role, was hopelessly Gay, and therefore quite harmless company; or, if not completely, if she felt like it, she might enjoy seducing him, knowing he doted on her looks, her notoriety as a sweet talker, or some sort of a 'femme fatale'. But only in style, not reality.

After the party, in fact during the reception, she started growing tired of all the eyes on her, and the foolish redundant questions about her role from rich new potential producers whose stares rolled down her unbelievable figure like sweat, or tears. What she knew the black Armani dress she wore would produce, was intended to produce, though not completely for her pleasure, but more her survival in this business where to age into a woman in her fifties was to lose. So it made sense to build up an image-bank one could draw on with those who might wait years before fulfilling their desires with her, which in turn could sustain her ego and career.

Instead of donning her dark glasses and annoying her press agent who disliked it—and was always handing out cards and setting up meetings she had no interest in right now, contented with the balance in her account after the obscene deposit she had just made—she had braved the publicity, unable to believe she had not outgrown being shy before the paparazzi and the awe-struck stares at her birthright beauty: the way she shifted her eyes, threw back her light-gold shoulder length hair with salon-set scallops, the way she pursed her beveled lips when making one of those glib put-downs or frank insights about someone's (usually male) presumed opinion of her; put-downs which she had based on nothing really at all, just another opportunity to act, to perfect lines that came to her spontaneously, and to which her interlocutor, taken aback by her presumptive defense, was unable to muster an equally witty reply.

Yes, during the reception she had agreed to spend a few days at the suburban Toronto home of the young actor's parents, who of course were thrilled to host such a beautiful actress they had seen on TV talk shows (if not her films), and whose very bashful or humble demeanor was propelling her, paradoxically, into fame among young women. After the suburban stay she planned to take a room at a posh downtown Toronto hotel, and the Canadian would drive her into the city and those clubs where an L.A. photographer had mentioned the ubiquitous subject of her memory and search (whose paintings he had once photographed), could be found, even if not without his present notorious lover, or mistress, she had been briefed about.

It was not the sort of interest or intimacy she wanted to discuss or share with any of her female peers. And there were a number whose company she enjoyed, whose company she needed; in fact had even been on intimate terms with, in that way that remained mysterious to most men, except what they saw in pornographic magazines and films, as far as she was concerned, which could never capture or communicate that special inner feminine closeness, pleasure, and fickleness they as women felt among themselves. Yet she had never told any of these female peers of her…what? She couldn't decide what it was now…what word would be best for it…whatever it was that she felt about him. It couldn't be just nostalgia for that past 'Flower Children' or 'Counter Culture' era when they had first met about forty years ago? If it was, then why didn't she continue to pursue so many of those other guys she had met back then, and even slept with at least once? Maybe that was it: if she had slept with that nut, if he had taken a hint and just guided her back to her pad in the 'Village' of Yorkville in Toronto and 'balled' her good she wouldn't be feeling continually like this now in her mid-fifties!

Or maybe he wasn't really attracted to her? Why hadn't she asked herself that before? Was it vanity all these years, the supreme if played down motivation in her cinematic worth and talent, that had been leading her on this one-sided obsession? What did she want anyway? Maybe he would ask her that if she ever had the guts to confront him and probably get quietly dismissed as someone he couldn't remember well; someone who found her interest charming and touching but that was all, and would move along simply bemused. But something kept telling her no, that would not happen, couldn't happen. Why not? Well, although she was rich and he wasn't, she still couldn't answer that. Or maybe it was because he was black? Or at least 'black' in the sense that her American society interpreted those who it was plain to see also had European ancestry, as was clear about him, yet in their North American parlance must be either one race or the other, since her 'people' had put such a premium on their skin, their hair, their features, that wherever it had mixed, blended, gelded (call it what you will) with another's skin or features, the result had to be denied, first by themselves (they reasoned), since such an occurrence must surely be anomalous, taking into account the over-stressed one-sided historical power arrangements, and abuse of slavery? Or even if today such results were willing on both sides, then that too would have to be an anomalous decision denying the concocted prestige of one side (we all know which) lending itself to the lesser other side?

The result was that she knew, or had encountered no 'black' Americans who obviously with a large visible amount of her race in them, could admit or acknowledge it as a normal fact which made their self-definition 'black', little more than a metaphor for their identity's continued (paradoxical) definitive manipulation by her race.

It was one of the reasons she had not mentioned anything about him to close girlfriends and fellow actresses, like Jenny Jong and Christene Carter. Suddenly, when she thought of them in relation to him, they were no longer her close friends she could confide anything about him to. They were 'Americans'. She wanted to think: 'too American', knowing herself the same presumptions, conclusions, fears, guilts, they had protected and deluded themselves with for generations, from any deep encounter with blacks, men especially. It always seemed too complicated, too sensitive an area to step into from their already complicated lives, and the roles they found themselves playing on screen; not really wanting to sometimes, but it was a job (winning the audition), so they must have had some inner cohesion, some subconscious suitability for the role? And they would end up never really being sure if it was simply a role they were playing as professional actresses, or just being their true selves? She, at least, wasn't one of those who cared to distribute herself in endlessly diverse 'character' roles, like a perfect schizoid machine, rather than explore the truth of herself in role after role.

Jenny, she knew, had started out un-jaded with touching roles as working girls looking for a better life in New York or L.A., without developing into Film Noirish 'femme fatales'. But then suddenly she started winning auditions for roles in which she was a champion of the underdog: the misunderstood, framed black ghetto youth, discriminated against because of his exceptional talent at basketball or debating controversial issues; the persecuted Korean shopkeeper; the deprived Hilly-Billy single mother and her little son with a speech impediment, etc. On screen Jenny would be like the lawyer (her own real life of course in shambles) for their defense, their caretaker, despite her stressful big-city day job and the impatience of a carefree boyfriend, and so on and so forth. The 'reality' of Jenny's screen roles seemed obvious, but they always excused her from any real-life involvements with non-whites; especially non-Americans, since she had already been involved with them on screen.

So she couldn't, she wouldn't, for a while anyway, tell Jenny about her old secret crush on the ubiquitous South American whose name she loved, and in preparation for her latest film, Summer Salt, had casually suggested as a name for a small witty black male role the script-writer had in mind. They had taken her suggestion. So there he was, in one of her films already, and no one knew who she was really thinking of whenever she called his name so romantically on screen! There were rumors…of course. And Jenny and Christene had brought up the subject over lunch in one of those exclusive restaurants they had a reserved table at in Studio City. Christene was the one whose roles, based on trendy singers or dancers (she was trained as a dancer and could move like the best of them) made her the target of all sorts of over-confident men who had seen what they wanted in her flickering screen image and weren't going to ignore the reality. Christene liked to call their bluff… if it was bluff; if not, they had to be hot to trot on the spot!

Christene had asked, leaning over her crab salad and chilled glass of Seven Daughters, the bottle in a sweating ice-cold gold bucket beside them: "So who's he? Do we know him?" Her response: a wag of the head and a little smile, eyes averted. They had no idea he was the artist of those zesty unfathomable abstract paintings she kept bringing back from somewhere or other, and which they admired over at her Malibu beach-house. "Ok, he's in the bullpen bracket, right?" Christene continued. Whaaat! You're way off! She didn't say, but thought, and Christene still on the hunt added: "So what's all the hush-hush about girl?…Oh I get it, he's…he's…black?"

That's it. She was definitely not crossing that line. No comment. Oh, awright, let me carry it on a bit, she decided after a few seconds, liking the topic anyway. "Oh he's an old friend I haven't seen in a long time." "But he nailed you good back when!" Christene had to add. "I wish!" she said. "Oh, one of those misses." Christene concluded, her voice loosing enthusiasm, its tone declining like a deflating tire, as she plunged her fork into a bundle of greens, shredded carrots and crabmeat, then with all that at its held up end, adding: "But you won't hold out on us when..." and with that left unsaid, she stuck the full fork between two pearly white even rows of teeth surrounding the pink cavern of her mouth, never finishing her sentence, but implying when the topic had become boring. And that was that.

She was trying to gradually slip unnoticed out of the hallway of this exclusive floor in an exclusive building on 5Th Avenue, where during some summers she had access to a posh two bedroom apartment on one of its upper floors which offered a

serene view of Central Park. She had already signaled to one of
the building's plain clothes security men, a short gentlemanly
but tough Sicilian, her intention to get out, even though she
heard herself agreeing over the cocktail buzz to do a cover shoot
and visually laid out centerfold article on her present life and
career in a week's time; having to explain to her new agent, who
was an energetic ever-optimistic go-getter woman in her thirties,
that she was taking a week out of town, and could she have all
the bouquets sent up to her apartment, which was in care of the
new agent.

So everything was set, the Canadian actor would pick her
up tomorrow evening and they would catch a small one hour
Delta flight to Toronto, to be whisked off to his parents suburban
home. In a day or two she would take one of the King Edward's
spacious single rooms on Toronto's King Street, which she
would book in advance by phone in the morning.

She was nibbling liver pate on a crisp whole wheat wafer
in her left hand while holding a half glass of very chilled
MacMurray Ranch Pinot in her right. She was nodding and
smiling while squeezing her way over to two groups of actors,
actresses, directors, cinematographers, and crew members
who were enjoying their success while it lasted. There was
no way she could vanish without being hugged, kissed, and
complimented by Gene O'Neil and Mitch Monroe, her two
male co-stars in Summer Salt, in which she had played a career
actress undecided about her choice between two suitors, played
by Gene and Mitch. But it wasn't they, but her, who was drawing
the crowds, especially young and over-thirty career women,
across North America and Europe as well, according to early
reports. She wondered if all these fans knew this film was really
a slightly modified remake of Otto Preminger's Daisy Kenyon,
of 1947, with Joan Crawford, Dana Andrews, and Henry Fonda,

which was remade again in the 1960s with Nathalie Wood. Her film had dropped that title completely while adjusting its plot to the social environment and values of L.A. in 2008. Personally she preferred 47s Daisy Kenyon to her film and the Nathalie Wood remake; but that was a secret never shared with anyone. She had probably won the audition because she saw the ghost of a liberated Joan Crawford—whom she revered—haunting the script's outline of her role. And now she wondered: Was it really a role, or just a large part of the truth about her life, which was still romantically unattached? Unlike Gene and Mitch, whose wives were right there in the party's gay crowd, keeping low profiles, probably out of suspicion that both their husbands had shown indiscretions while on the job, which as wives they no doubt appreciated, since they too had their own discreet little side-trips from time to time.

The whole affair, she mused unperturbed, was like checks and balances to marital lows, which helped it to rebound. So whose idea was it anyway that Gene, Mitch, and herself should end up in bed with each-other, separately that is, in between scenes? She couldn't remember, and didn't care. Though the actual remembered escapades made her laugh silly in Gene and Mitch's company now, blushing as they each eyed her, smiled, and even touched her. She remembered the difference between them as not having anything to do with their ability in bed, but hers: her pillow-fluffed insides which she offered from one to the other, whenever she felt like taking a relaxed short cut, a sort of 'dress rehearsal' through the prosaic demands of the script. And they caught on to that too, though it was herself who benefited most it seemed, because the role was also her real life, whereas they were 'acting', because they were already attached as real-life marital partners.

Their arrival at Toronto's Pearson International Airport was not as anonymous as they had thought it would be. Not that she was annoyed or surprised. She was just prone to these lapses where she forgot that the news media—the magazines and those idiotic half-hour programs with doll-like hostesses speaking in rapt tones, alternating with young male hosts trying to look as nonchalant as possible with their hands in the pockets of odd suits bought off a rack rather than tailored to fit, their hair damp and striated like a busy wharf rat's fur—had given her another identity, and she was no longer just a woman on a flight. Her recognition began at JFK, in stops and starts, according to how long it took for people of both sexes, from teens up, to recognize her. After all she was on at least one of those magazine covers shining in nauseous gloss on one of the Airport's kiosk's racks.

One thing she always liked as a professional on flights associated with New York, Toronto, and L.A. was the latent excitement, as though something had been accomplished or was going to be accomplished. This feeling ran through her like a flash of lightening, and rippled when she thought of him whom she hadn't laid eyes on for about five years, when she had last flown into Toronto for a film festival, and had no time for anything extra because she was on a tight agenda, all the more forgettable (except for the money it had helped her make) because she had found the old spacious downtown cinema venues gone, torn down; those that had made the festival exciting and popular in the first place, rather than a status event. They had been replaced by a few Cineplexes, institutional auditoriums, and concert halls for the Festival's program. The young people in charge of the festival quite programmatic, affected, making much ado about nothing, asking her silly obscure questions at press conferences. She had left in forty-eight hours. But not before snooping information about him from a few Toronto art fans who knew who he was, knew he had made an impression—or rather, had been allowed to make a public impression, at least once, on important figures interested in the multi-cultural history of the city since the 1970s, and now was regarded in that Andy Wahrol fifteen-minutes-of-fame manner, as just another eccentric has-been. One who could be found basking in the summer sun in small parks surrounding exclusive U of T libraries, where he seemed to have Carte Blanche by being nothing more than a harmless crank.

And sure enough she had found him—having suggested an outdoor stroll with friends—exactly as one of the festival committee members had predicted, sitting on a park bench in the early afternoon, suavely dressed as usual, graying at the temples, in white slacks, a pale turquoise shirt revealing his hairless terracotta brown chest beneath a chocolate brown Issey Miyake wind coat, cream espadrilles, smoking a small cigar while gazing into space, or wherever, a copy of the New York Review of Books folded and partly visible in a plastic bag beside him on the bench, oblivious to her of course, who walked by protected by Lolita Limpeca dark glasses in the company of her agent, and producer of the film she was about to begin shooting in L.A. after flying out of Toronto that evening for London to discuss another script with the intended young English director she had already worked with, and in whose company she would probably fly back to Hollywood. And as his luck would have it (sometimes she wondered if he wasn't pretending he had no idea what was going on around him?) she overheard a few art history university students (bespectacled young women in black with tote bags on their shoulders), who were standing on a paved pathway dissected by a large vertical metallic sculpture apparently influenced by Vladmir Tatlin, mention his first name, adding the name of some London gallery that had recently contracted him. She had silently took note of this, not even bringing up the topic to her two companions who were busy ironing out the issue of the film budget, so that in London she knew exactly what gallery to find, found it and his shocking new canvasses of soft weather-beaten tones. She bought two, which, staring at them in her London hotel room before she left, had put her in a strange invigorating creative mood on the flight back to L.A., when not dozing off under the effect of pressed Chicken breast with a handful of raviolis in pesto sauce, and two glasses of chilled white Ferrari-Cerano.

Passengers in the little Delta airbus, which had no real First Class, probably thought they were a couple, the young Canadian actor and her. She didn't mind, though she thought he acted a bit nervous, after all she didn't look her age, she looked in her thirties, at least twenty years younger than she was. It wasn't so easy to pull off, but she liked the film business because it kept her fit and ahead of the upcoming competition. And so she kept going, having never had a child, and still no cellulite, even though when she felt hot flashes and dryness she confronted it with generous doses of Damaina leaf, milkshakes with brewers yeast, lots of apple-cider and yogurt.

She had made herself what she was and felt great about it, pushing her shades up over the flounces of her red-gold hair hiding streaks of grey, a hairstyle she was proud to continue from Monica Vitti in L'avventura, watching the Canadian immigration officer check his screen, giving him that mischievous bold grin which emphasized the perfect evenness and polished porcelain sheen of her teeth beneath her fearless blue-grey eyes. The immigration officer quickly slipping her passport back saying: "You're all set", while she imagined him checking the Toronto Star's illustrated cinema listings for her films from now on, walking away with a wide smooth experienced sway in a pair of slim black high heels which went nicely with the Armani close-fitting silver satin pantaloons covered with mauve, emerald green, yellow and orange flowery pastel designs, like its close-fitting matching waist-high jacket.

They left Pearson whisked away at the back of a limousine. Soon they were sliding along the lanes, the underpasses, the detours illuminated by pools of multi-colored lights in a cool breeze. Before long she was feeling securely lost in the flat suburban stillness, the strange silence of the house and neighborhood, putting on her silk pajamas, turning in, determined to think of him, whose presence in the city had brought her here. And suddenly she hit on the idea that she wanted to return to Yorkville, not to shop as she had done on other trips while in a completely different frame of mind, but to deliberately see the same streets, the same locations, the same houses, even the same house perhaps—if it was still there—where she had stayed in the summer of 1970, Toronto's Summer of Love, when she was fifteen, and had embraced him.

The same day she moved into her room at King Edward—loving the roaring sound of heavy red and white streetcars on King Street below—she went down to Yorkville with her young Canadian host and actor, who had picked her up in his black Lexus sports. They used a small parking lot she never remembered being there. Neither had been the restaurants flanking it, one in the same spot where she knew for sure the 'Darcys' nightclub had stood, the only and most popular black dancing club uptown, to her knowledge, where she had seen him a few times in the frontline outside, among gorgeous hip black Southern 'chicks' who had blown into town with their long flowing see-through dresses, their fluffy uncombed shampooed Afros, their baubles, bangles, and beads shaking rhythmically when they flung their hips around jamming him, on nimble feet with orange-painted toenails while snapping their fingers to

Booker T & The MGs "Hiphugher," or Martha Reeves & the
Vandellas "Jimmy Mack," or "Uptight" by Stevie Wonder, or
"Rescue Me" by Fontella Bass. She saw him blowing a reefer
one time with a certain short dark girl whose rusty kinky hair
touched his as she whispered something in his ear and they broke
up laughing in that restrained spasmodic stoned way, while the
crowd she stood in gelled and shunted on the packed pave of
'love children' outside 'Darcy's', and the young cops on the beat
turned a blind eye to the lit reefers and pungent smoke mixed
with perfumed incense and the exotic fragrance of Oriental
flower oils on the probably un-bathed skins of hippies.

She wondered, but doubted if he knew that today that
same Afro-American girl, whose vivacious style she realized
fascinated him, as it did her who had felt jealous, left out,
unable to even compete with their private ethnic familiarity...
she wondered if he knew that same girl was a leading Jazz-Pop
singer today, who, like her, had enough money to appear half her
age. In fact, they had been casual friends way back then, when
she became aware that he, the dark girl's so-called 'brother', in
his frontier brown suede vest, silver Moroccan shirt, slim maroon
corduroy trousers and Beatle boots, in that elusive, euphoric,
and altruistic mood of the times, had been attractive to her, a
white 'teeny-bopper', in the same way she knew a quiet music-
oriented 'Head' from Tennessee, with shoulder length black hair
and a face like Rory Calhoun, whom she knew well, had been
attractive to the very Afro-American girl, his so-called 'sister',
who danced, smoked, and laughed with him, but without the
same apparent sexual attraction she had for the quiet long haired
hip white music lover.

She was lost in thoughts like these which she came to the
'Village' to revive, and did, standing in her blue jeans, grey
t-shirt, and light calf-skin cowboy boots on the pave looking

down that short trendy avenue between Yorkville and Bloor Street, at the end of which she could see that the old popular Embassy Tavern—where they all drifted after they were high, their throats dry, to sit around ice-cold draft at forty cents a glass—had obviously been torn down, replaced by a shiny stone structure that was no doubt another designer fashion outlet.

A lot of Yorkville Ave had remained the same though; renovated no doubt, except that the little houses were no longer in their bright colors and had evolved into fashion and gadget stores. But that portion of raised slanted sidewalk with flat inlaid pieces of stone was still there, she was thrilled to see. It was where all the popular 'Heads', dressed like royal hybrids: half Native Indian half cowboy; half African tribesman half safari hunter; half 18th century cavalier half Oriental sheik; half Parisian courtesan half suffragette; half frontier pioneer woman half gypsy girl; half cotton-picking slave woman half Egyptian princess ... had sat briefly in the summer twilight, pulling recognized friends down beside them, giggling high-spirited. He, she, their friends, their speech punctuated with phrases like: "Sure thing," "I'm hip," "That's cool," "It's a shaky scene," "What a bummer!" etc.

Now she saw a few somber-looking Latin American immigrants (or refugees?), selling colorful skillfully woven wrist bands, sashes, and nice jewelry. She bought a few wrist bands and metal bracelets, which she would wear tonight with the rest of her intended sloppy unnoticeable appearance when she went in search of 'him'. The gay actor also suggested she top it off with a Blue Jays baseball cap, which they picked up later at a gift shop before reaching the corner of Yorkville and Hazelton. It felt impossible to visualize again what she had experienced here with 'him', whose actual presence she had a sudden desperate desire to renew, as though to hold on to something that must have meant something. After all it had lasted so long, vanished then returned, yet here at this corner it had all began.

She could not see herself in the present any longer, could not fathom why that night forty years ago she had worn that silky almost transparent long dress and the little black beret, with a flower behind one ear, and nothing else, except her glittering beige and cream fine bead necklace. The young actor walked with her up Hazelton to Scollard, a short corner away, from which she kept staring up the remainder of Hazelton, but had no real desire to find or see the tall three-storied house where she had lodged in the summer of '70. Nothing she cherished had happened there. The action had always been on Yorkville Avenue itself, 'where it was at', back in '70. And now she felt a hot flash (was it the end of her fertility or its second Spring?) between her legs when a vivid picture of that night returned, and where among the throngs of 'beautiful people' she had seen him in his black hat with a Jaguar skin band, coming down from Avenue Road with the tall bearded Jewish 'Head' from Kentucky, the lanky tall good-looking colored one from Detroit, in his slanted black hat ringed by silver conchos, like Jimi Hendrix, and the other pale one from Toronto, with his hair always well brushed like a girl's, bouncing on his shoulders, and a face like Edmund Purdom.

Her two 'teeny-bopper' girlfriends from San Francisco like herself, who had driven all the way up to New York's Greenwich Village, then across the border in a flower painted Volkswagon controlled by their actual brothers, before coming over to Yorkville in Toronto, had stood with her across the street, and one had said: "There's Andy, isn't he cute? I hear he raps all the time about those way-out writers my brother talks about, like Baudelaire and Nerval and Thoreau." And there he was on the curb of Yorkville and Hazelton with his fingers stuck in the front pockets of his tight red corduroy jeans, one silver Oriental bracelet on each wrist, bare feet in Indian leather sandals, a silvery collarless Moroccan silk shirt beneath one of those snug thin brown glossy nylon windbreakers that came up to his waist. And she had felt a magnetic force pulling her across the avenue, so just like that she had walked across to him, her naked body swaying beneath the long silk dress like a night gown, and the black beret pulled across her long red-gold hair split at her shoulders and falling to her sharp little breasts.

She had hugged him abruptly so that he could remember her body beneath the soft material pressed up against his, then quickly pulled back her head with a broad smile, looking into his brown face and matching eyes, which seemed merely pleased and understanding, as though what she had done was the normal thing to do. All he had said was: "What's happenin'?" in that deep familiar tone of voice, as though they were old friends. Then he and his buddies were off again, lost among the crowd on the sidewalk, their voices continuing some conversation they were deeply engrossed in which her presence had interrupted briefly.

While she visualized all this, the young Canadian who was born in the eighties after every trace of the Yorkville summer of love had vanished, was commenting on this and that about the present owners of the boutiques, restaurants, and the 'who's who' professionals in studios concerned with architecture and publishing in the Village today. But she wasn't really hearing anything, yet being experienced in the game of listening and agreeing to projects that often never got off the ground—like the piles of scripts she received continually, most of which she thought were rubbish derived from the same writing courses with break-down strategies to keep audiences breathing hard and literally jumping in their seats while munching buckets of popcorn—she kept smiling and nodding.

It was not until he walked her across Yorkville Avenue

towards a shopping and outdoor café lane that she mentioned how anxious she was, even scared, sort of, to see him again, adding she wanted to be there at the club the young actor said he was sure to visit tonight, since apparently it was owned by one of his mistress' girl friends. She wanted to be there inconspicuously before he arrived.

And that was their last relaxed moment, because people, young women especially, clearly dressed in fashion from the boutiques in the area, their cell phones going off every five minutes in their brand name handbags, were beginning to stare at them; stop, look back, and she knew what was coming, so dug into her Vuitton handbag for her Pilot pen and had it in her hand ready, before the young actor, realizing they had been spotted— or rather: she had been spotted—started stammering to the effect that this was indeed true. And all she said was: "So? Let's work on that damn film! C'mon help me with them!" before the first bold star-gazer with dark shades up on her teased frizzy strawberry colored head asked: "Aren't you Laura Garson?" not even waiting for a reply as she fumbled for her address book, opened it at double blank pages, and watched "Laura Garson, best wishes!" scrawled across both pages expertly. Another fan, apparently more into film history, and about half Laura's age—as were most of them who began to gather—blurted out: "Aren't you related to the great actress Greer Garson?" And of course she nodded affirmatively, but her smile betrayed mostly mischievousness since the little dear hadn't realized Laura Garson wasn't her real name anyway. Another with a sort of look like Liza Minnelli and a curious commercial frame of mind asked: "Is this your first time in Yorkville? How do you find it?" And she panicked, because the whole secret of her visit suddenly felt threatened in a clairvoyant moment. Quick, say something! "Oh it's fine here, you have a lovely city!" And she felt a little funny since the questioner hadn't produced anything for her to autograph! She shot a glance at the young actor whom no one had even bothered with, and he realized she needed to edge out now because a crowd was beginning to gather and the lane they were in was blocked. She began to feel sweat rising to the surface of her face from the roots of her hair, just as the young actor managed to say: "Ok Ok Miss Garson has to do some other things, thank you!" But one really grungy young girl with torn jeans, a ring in one nostril, and half-turquoise half-maroon hair plastered to her skull, asked cynically: "Is this film you're flogging, what's it called? Summer Salt? Or whatever, really as good as they're making out?" And she answered automatically, without hesitation, because that was the first question that woke up her reputation as a smart talker: "Well, aren't all somersaults supposed to be good?" And that had them silent for a second or two, before her pun's cryptic ice thawed, and a few of them started to laugh, then all of them, some going: "Wow!" and another: "You got that right girl!" and another: "I hear yah!"

And with that the young actor got her out the other end of the lane and across Cumberland Street, where they hurried through another narrow lane between a Cineplex and a high rise, not even stopping to gaze at the glossy poster for Summer Salt, which they glanced at in a framed Plexiglas box above their heads in the laneway; Laura Garson almost bursting out laughing at the silly poster of herself striking a pose between Gene O'Neill and Mitch Monroe, which was nothing like those vintage old Hollywood posters she loved, religiously collected, and bought coffee table books about.

He led her through the passage way towards Bloor Street, all the while yapping about the anxieties, the favors, the insults, the come-ons he had experienced on the set, in some sort of sudden awakening of his professional conscience the scenario they had left behind must have suddenly awakened. Busy Bloor Street reminded her a bit of 6ᵗʰ Avenue's (Avenue of the Americas) narrower part in New York, which she could still see. They walked past Chapters bookstore, Starbucks, and began to pick up pace when they saw lingering stares of recognition. They went past 'The Body Shop', then 'Emporio Armani', turned the corner at Bay outside David's, passed the Bay subway entrance and got through the short crowd-less block which brought them back to Yorkville Avenue and the car park, from which he drove her back to her hotel on King Street.

It must have been the impossibility of being anonymous again that made Laura Garson stand at a curtained window in her hotel room that evening and imagine it a pleasure to be anyone on the sidewalk of narrow Victoria Street below. But it was just a fleeting feeling. She couldn't have ended up with a better life, she realized. So why was she so bent on pursuing this guy, which she realized now had become such an addiction it could not be hidden that well? The young actor who was now her accomplice, she suspected was also gaily thrilled to help with her 'cruising'. What was he, this flamboyant painter and film fan, to her, if not just another old acquaintance she felt stuck on because his difference in origin, and the fact that he wasn't 'big enough', had held her back from going all the way into that loose intimacy she had squandered on so many others?

Or was it the other way round? She was waiting for him to notice her, make the first move to prove that this wasn't a one-sided affair in which she didn't exist? She wondered if he was the substitute child—even an adopted one—she had never had? Naaw! She never went for any of that Freudian shrink stuff! But maybe there was some truth to desired sex at least? Well, why the hell not! Oh she could hear some saying it was just the same old 'black sheep' process she had reserved for him after all she had done with others. Well, who cares, the proof will be in the pudding, and he might like it!

Was that it, really? Hell, no! Maybe he was the real one, the true one? It was a comforting thought at least, and she had to smile, remembering that tape she had heard, which some Gay neurotic tenant had secretly taped of him making love… no… fucking (she could tell the difference even if he couldn't!) that same sly freaky bitch who would probably arrive with him tonight at some club she would be taken to! That clandestine pirated tape had turned her on, no doubt about it…if he could do that with his 'mistress' why not her too? She knew him long before that freaky airhead anyway!

She flopped down on a soft easy chair facing the half open window with a view towards Front Street and giggled silly when she remembered what she had heard about the real intended use of that tape: how the Gay tenant had glorified him as some Gaylord and played the tape at a perfectly real pitch while he (the Gay tenant) was being sodomized in the bedroom of an adjacent apartment in their partitioned house. Meanwhile, the poor painter home alone next door (as he was supposed to be), as though punished for not being Gay himself, would be going clean out of his mind when he heard his freaky girlfriend's voice soaring in ecstasy, but wouldn't believe it was himself creating it! Since the gay cyclist who used his friend's place next door never played the tape when she was at home with him.

That reminded her…she dialed her private two storied apartment building in L.A. on her Blackberry to check up on how everything was going with her younger sister and her Afro girlfriend, both of whom she allowed to live rent free in the spacious bottom flat, with the agreement that they would keep an eye on her huge luxurious top flat when she was away, which could often be for months. Then she phoned Alphonso, the caretaker of her Malibu beach house, and reminded him to thoroughly clean the sand that blew up on its glass windows, and stuck to the polished floor. She lay back in a soft comfortable upholstered chair and rested her bare feet on a matching stool. She had already informed the hotel restaurant to send up her chicken salad with cucumber Gazpacho, a slice of Lasagna, and a glass of Eddy's slow churn low fat chocolate ice cream, at 4 pm. In the meantime she took out one of the scripts her agent had given her, swung both bare feet over the side of the chair, and checked to see what was considered the latest hot property in Hollywood.

She had no idea which part of downtown Toronto they were in when they parked in a diagonal side street, walked back a bit and climbed the stairs to a club over-looking the same diagonal street. She had napped well, but hadn't taken a bath, reserving that for when she got in with the intention of staying in bed until ten or eleven am at least, then maybe even bringing forward her flight back to New York a few days, anticipating the increased pulse of her professional mileau pumping up the extravagant self-pride she would apply to her scheduled cover-photo interview with 'Vanity Fair' when she got back.

No one was supposed to even guess such a life applied to her when she walked into the club in blue jeans, Kerry sneakers, a grey t-shirt, her hair in a pony-tail under a Blue Jays cap, and some colorful South American woven and metallic wrist bands on her left hand. The third finger of which would also brandish a cheap gold ring to ward off any horny one-night-standers. Her young male Canadian companion almost looked the same except that his hair was cut short. Not until they were climbing the stairs did he mention that in fact the club was in a flexible 'Gay' area of the city, and she suddenly wondered aloud about her expected…was he….? Not really, her chaperon said, in a tone critical or disappointed, but the girl he was living with was, he added, apparently delighted .Poor guy! She was dying to see how knowing or not knowing all this had affected his demeanor, his behavior, his apparent indifference or detachment, which she remembered had always fascinated her about him.

They had arrived at around 9.30pm, time enough to see his arrival and avoid being seen arriving conspicuously themselves. They sat at the bar which was at the end of a large room, but gave a good view of the club's floor filled with tables and chairs diagonally arranged. What thrilled her was the presence of a perfectly working vintage Wurlitzer at the middle of the room, against a side wall, whose window overlooked the quiet side street below. What further thrilled her were the 45s from the 70s and 80s they saw in the Wurlitzer's list of tunes when they went over to check it out as Fleetwood Mac's "Lies" filled the room's atmosphere. What thrilled her again was the young actor mentioning matter-of-factly that he heard her expected friend was a fan of the club mainly because of that nostalgic Wurlitzer.

They were sitting at a corner of the bar which gave a clear view across the floor and the top of the stairs where a short red head in a boy-cut, a studded tight black shirt with slanted cut off sleeves at the shoulder like a Samourai's vest, and white shorts exposing her slim shapely legs, stood greeting everyone warmly, as though she already knew each of them. She was thinking how the whole place felt incongruent with her conception, her definition, her memory, or whatever it was she thought of him. He would always be that enigmatic distant stranger whose silver shirt and bracelets shone in a perfumed colorful crowd of long-haired, moustached youths on Yorkville's packed sidewalk on summer's nights in 1970. They had all changed of course, herself probably more than many she had known; especially those who were left stuck in a sort of time-warp which turned them into guinea-pigs for every new drug, their battered minds barely hanging on to the lifelines of reality which came in the form of short-time jobs and welfare checks. She had taken her share of such help long ago, but never eased up on viewing films at the repertoire cinemas in L.A. and San Francisco and Berkeley, reading avidly, taking a few dramatic night classes after her daytime supermarket job, and keeping fit. Her sharp but short recollection of him had leapt to twice its size when she had first realized that he too had made their crazy years pay off, and turned into a fairly successful painter. But this club wasn't the sort of place which reminded her of him. There was an atmosphere of shady hustling about it, more tolerated than intended probably, as though the guys and dolls filling up the tables after acknowledging the duck-haired gypsy-looking bartender, were on the prowl for a hustle disguised as a good time. She couldn't help thinking of that bar in the Film Noir classic Phantom Lady, and herself in the role Ella Raines played as 'Kansas', the loyal secretary out to prove her boss's innocence.

"You're missing your lover boy," the young actor was saying. They were sipping their Vermouths on the rocks, and she had been looking across the bar at the faces of some of the slick well-dressed middle-aged loners, who had probably taken their regular seats there. The bartender leaned forward and said something briefly in a low tone to one of the loners, who nodded before the bartender looked her way. It was the sort of behavior that she noticed quickly from experience. When she looked at the top of the stairs a small-boned well-shaped woman with a small, yes, pretty face which somehow reminded her of Virginia Mayo, or better yet, Veronica Lake, with golden-pink skin that she could see from her position was also freckled, stood there. On her jet black silky hair flowing past her shoulders almost to her waist, was a slanted green beret. That struck her as a little odd, and was an irritant. The girl wore a brown silk shirt that stopped just above the elastic waist of grey Cotton Ginny flannel breeches. She had one of those small colorful Chinese purses made out of silk slung across her modest chest, and wore flat little magenta Chinese shoes. The young woman with the beret seemed quite chummy with the young hostess; they were hugging and whispering into each-other's ears at the top of the stairs.

It came as a surprise to realize he was the guy who had come in with her because he had moved so silently and quickly away from her. He was dressed in grey espadrilles somewhat matching the cream jeans he wore with a long-sleeved horizontally striped black and red jersey. His body looked the same as when she last saw him; in fact he looked quite fit, which made his graying uncombed husky head of hair, matching his moustache and low beard, contradict his apparent youthfulness, since she knew like her he was on the second half of his 50s. He sat in one of the four chairs at a round table in a corner behind the wall which hid the stairs. They were in a diagonal about twenty feet away from each other, but she made sure her eyes met his. This lasted a few seconds before a brown-skinned girl with a high creole accent sat in a chair opposite him and blocked her view of his face. They had arrived with a small entourage apparently; the girl with the beret—his girl the actor whispered in her ear—followed by another creole girl of lighter completion and a voluptuous body highlighted by white shorts and a militant green khaki shirt with regimental color bars, a current fashion style, on its front pockets.

"Lover boy indeed! Picasso, Modigliani, and Toulouse Lautrec all rolled into one!" the young actor continued quietly, smiling at her.

"Oh shut up!" she whispered jovially, cutting her eyes with a glance in the artist's direction.

His girl with the beret didn't seem to like the table he had chosen, she kept looking over her shoulder to other tables closer to the center of the room, and to the bar. Laura Garson was afraid. In any case those tables were filling up with guys who had Caribbean accents, including East Indian guys who seemed to be in the expatriate high salary bracket. The girl with the beret seemed to know them all, even more than the artist did. He was the one giving a doting barmaid orders that applied beyond their table. His girl took a pouch of Drum tobacco and a sheaf of Rizla papers from her purse and proceeded to roll herself a cigarette. The artist was apparently pleasing the barmaid dressed in a short skirt like a High School student, which revealed a generous amount of her not bad at all legs. His girl was talking, joking, smiling in a cryptic way with three of the colored Caribbean guys, who were dressed in that popular style of bright sweat shirts, zipped up hooded wind breakers, and khaki fatigues with big pockets on the legs. One was saying to her in a teasing jovial tone exaggerated by his convoluted ascent: "I hear, seh, Sally can't dance." She had lit up by now and replied while smoke oozed through her narrow nostrils and thin lips pulled to the side: "Where were you? Jerking off?" Everybody cracked up. But not the artist, he simply smiled, reached for the bag of tobacco and rolled himself a cigarette. Before he did this Laura Garson had sworn their eyes met and recognition ignited, sparked, for a second at least, since the creole girl opposite him and between them had left her chair abruptly.

But now was not the time for proof of their mutual recognition, she thought. What she felt sure of was that he was no longer the whimsical, ethereal, enigmatic mute she had met over three dozen years ago. Sure, he still had that distant reclusive air, but it didn't strike her as pleasant, like before. He was alienated from the very circle he socialized in. He had become part of a specie, it seemed, that's all. He had no individuality left, only its remnants, like froth in his empty beer glass before him. The girl with the beret wouldn't permit it, Laura Garson decided, as if she too would have been the same, so she knew. The girl with the beret was like a queen of his species. Their queen, not his alone. She knew the role, she had been offered such thrones before. He had to get out to reclaim his real identity, she decided. His individual identity, the one she knew of. Laura Garson decided she would help. It was a decision that somehow felt more satisfying than everything she had already done secretly for him.

"I'm into him in a big way," the young barmaid was announcing to the bartender, about four or five yards down the bar from the actress and actor. "That bitch don't like me," the barmaid went on, "she knows her floppy disk can't play him like mine." The bartender guffawed and said: "It's good enough for a somersault in a while though," quietly reaching up to the wine glass rack above his head, then filling a glass with Le Piat D'or, and placing it on her tray. "That bitch," the barmaid muttered, swooping up some quarters from the bar and clattering them on her tray before walking over seductively to the artist's table.

The word 'somersault' had unnerved Laura Garson, who started pulling down the peak of her Blue Jays cap and lowering her eyes and face to the bar. The young actor didn't act as scared, even though they had exchanged glances upon hearing the word, which by the nonchalance of the bartender seemed an innocent coincidence, while the Wurlitzer played Stevie Wonder's "Part Time Lover". She asked the young actor if he thought they should leave shortly, after all he had to drive back to the suburbs and they shouldn't have too many drinks.

"What's this? You're not jealous are you?"
"I wish! Look, I don't even know the guy."
"Hey, look," he whispered, "Lover boy's coming over to us."

The artist had stood up and was making his way around the tables and across the floor. Laura Garson started fidgeting with her second glass of Vermouth, and muttered: "Oh Jesus." She held on to the arm of the actor in a romantic way and directed her gaze towards the bartender. She didn't see when the artist approached the Wurlitzer. She heard the ringing drop of a coin in the machine's mechanism, then a deep seductive sound, and looking over saw the Wurlitzer's key board light up red as each song was punched. She let go of the young actor's arm, and he said: "Called your bluff, didn't he?" Laura Garson smiled and said, "Let's hear his selections, then leave." Just then the girl with the beret swayed over to the Wurlitzer and like a sleek seductress grazed her broad hips against the artist's, hooked her left arm through his right, called him 'Baby,' and proceeded to deposit her coins, punching while the machine hummed and buzzed before the first selection, which was Toto's "Hold the Line," boomed out.

Laura Garson crossed her legs, sipped her Vermouth, and felt her imagination run wild as she tried to guess which tunes were his among: "Hot-Blooded," "Heart and Soul," "Stranded," "Bette Davis Eyes," and "Jump." The young actor and her spoke quietly of various professionals in the film industry who it would be important to keep in contact with; people she knew, and would recommend his name to. New patrons emerged at the top of the club's stairs, some dressed outrageously flashy, their behavior outlandish and spasmodic as though high. No one seemed to care. Over at the artist's table his girl had taken off her beret and was swinging her well kept black glossy mane, leaning back in her chair, all in response it seemed to being the star attraction. The artist seemed content with his beer, his rolled cigarette, the music, and being some sort of advisor to the clinging interest of the colored girl with the creole accent sitting at his side, who Laura Garson guessed was from his country of origin.

She had no idea when the artist's girlfriend vanished. It was only when the barmaid who had served their tables returned with her tray to the bar that she overheard her saying to the bartender: "So the 'Women' is occupied, only it's not all by women, but at least one male in a woman's wig! Isn't that bitch something?" The bartender, bending to snap glasses he was filling from bottles of Crème de Menthe and Brandy, muttered: "Mind your own business," and kept pouring.

Laura Garson decided she had seen and heard enough. She finished her Vermouth, and so did the young actor, like a silent efficient aide-de-camp beside her. They left an extra ten along with the twenty dollar tab, and she rapped on the bar to notify the bartender before heading across the floor, not unnoticed as before it seemed, since the heads of girls were turning to stare at her face. Well check this out! She heard a voice in her head saying before she stopped just for a few seconds across from the artist's table, where there was no mistaking this time their eyes met. She smiled just for another few seconds; a smile she knew had none of the determined meaning she had intended, but out of control rose to the surface of her face naturally from somewhere deep inside a past she had not lost. He looked at her as though he thought she were a ghost, yet his eyes were penetrating her flesh she felt, while his face seemed to relax with gratitude for those seconds before she vanished down the stairs.

"Jesus Christ, how did he get involved in that!" She said as if to herself, almost running down the stairs. The young actor replied: "I told you, didn't I?"

She caught a flight back to New York around 1pm the next day. An executive from her studio who was in Toronto had heard she was at the King Edward and sent a call through to her in the morning. They left together for New York, he helping her to get through Pearson International quicker with a few informed security officers. They went right through just in time to catch the last shuttle bus out to the small Delta on a sunny afternoon, and the mild stir she caused with her deliberately swinging hips, unkempt hair, dark glasses, body-hugging floral Armani silk pants and matching jacket, put her back in the mood for a hectic New York agenda.

She went shopping on 5th Avenue, then Madison. Bought an expensive sleek very short armless dress with a deep cleavage by Krizia; it was in fine netted relief stitching, and the color of golden sugar crystals. She had her arms, legs, and buttocks massaged with rose oil and buffed, then took the photos for her Vanity Fair interview. In the interview she made comments, hints, signifying her obscure relationship to 'him'—proven by references to roles like Deborah Kerr's in An Affair to Remember, and Nancy Kwan's in The World of Suzie Wong—but which the average reader would be unable to detect.

The way she lay back with her knees up on a sofa, half her thighs exposed, her stare of desire beyond the photographer's camera, was intended for 'him', the artist, to see, to read. She felt a deep-seated secret thrill thinking of him while doing the photo shoot.

FREEWAY

On a freeway this moment freezes. That's not the actual truth of course, but it feels that way because my cold hands resist the car's steering wheel on this precipice of the present. Stop! Or you'll slam into the blank wall of the sky! Some voice in my head says.

A bronze bridge sparkles like the spine of an exotic butterfly floating down into the metropolis…which turns out not to be there. Instead, the sudden appearance of dark water slapping a shore-line of broken, rotting, slimy branches. Then the amplified sound of those branches breaking, leaves crunching, that horrible snorting and heavy breathing coming from the monstrous heads of colossal green scaly creatures seen towering against the blue sky as they rip, chew, and swallow the top of fully grown trees.

This could be a story the 30 something engineer (working on this wild river bank's terrain), is writing (I haven't decided as yet…I may never decide) about a freeway bulldozing its way through neglected State land, intending to link up with the main highway several miles ahead, a highway flowing with traffic right now, like electricity rushing to be plugged into the metropolis appearing again beyond the bronze bridge, which sparkles like the spine of an exotic butterfly below a sky of slowly moving giant clouds resembling the ghosts of dinosaurs half submerged in dark water.

The antique tomahauk resting in its bed of white tissue paper in a shoebox on the seat beside him as he drives along this freeway, could have been used to smash the skull of someone like himself, in resistance to the plans of his fore parents to install their word of God as The Word of God here, so that he could succeed in owning this freeway, this car, this air space above, around, and below the earth. It's an interesting thought (but not better than the taste of these two warm apple strudel pastries just bought at a road side 7/11!) to pursue while on the freeway. And of course the 30 something engineer is already a past sentence, used up. But why should it be forgotten or deleted? This is not some lesson in story-telling; it just happens that I can't help thinking all this while driving along the freeway, and I'm telling you these thoughts in writing.

This 30 something is a man of conscience. It's not hurting that much, because of all the historical data he's consumed concerning the settlement of this land his magenta vintage model Chrysler PT Cruiser is dashing smoothly over now towards an apartment building with its brass-bordered glass doors, and its elevator to his apartment ten stories up, overlooking some, but dwarfed by other buildings along a busy avenue in the metropolis. In his bookcase up there are dozens of the latest published studies on cultures before his (but what is his? Or is THIS it?) that have been rethought, updated…and therefore as familiar now as the archaeological relic of the tomahauk lying in crinkled tissue paper in a shoebox on the free seat beside him.

What would Onika think of that tomahauk? Of course it would be what I think. I'm thinking about what I think Onika would, or should think, while driving to the end of this freeway which is nowhere in sight. Which is not true of course, but don't you dare turn this page or flip to the final fullstop when I haven't even braked and turned this motor off! I'm a reader too, and just as baffled as you.

Onika will keep us both interested to the end. I'm giving Onika

(I'm the writer, I can do that) to this 30 something guy sporting reddish uncut curling hair damp with sweat (it's summer) at his temples and on the nape of his neck. He's supposed to look like Chateaubriand in one of his early oil portraits. Hint: This man does not look like me, the writer. If this suddenly makes my text some confused exotic brand of specialized literature you need to take a crash course in, get to hell off my page!

Onika and I have something in common…or many things, but we weren't made for each other. Get that straight right now. So don't put us in prison for riding this freeway like runaways from whatever definition it is we're not supposed to be running away from.

We can see her up in the 30 something guy's apartment in the metropolis he's still driving towards with the tomahauk in the shoebox beside him. But this is maybe a year after they first sat side by side, by sheer chance one summer lunch break, on a stone bench along the short cobble-stone promenade leading to and from the tall edifice of MOMA fifty or sixty yards away. He had come down with his lunch—Tuna fish with mayo on rye, a vegetable salad with olives, shredded carrots, cucumber, broccoli, and tomatoes, with Italian dressing, and a take-out cappuccino— from the fifth floor office of an engineering firm he works for a few corners away. She had just walked around the block from a ladies boutique where she performed multiple duties as sales girl, model, and window dresser. A task she seemed suited for, since the boutique catered to those adventurous girls who wanted to look as though they were off on safari, or to see the pyramids of Egypt, or on a trip down the Amazon, in their khaki jackets, linen or cotton shirts, broad leather belts. Off to sleep in huts with mosquito nets, oil lamps, shotguns and quinine, like Clark Gable, Ava Gardner, and Grace Kelly in Mogambo, or Beverly Garland in a B cult film like Curucu, Beast of the Amazon, or that other one: Creature From the Black Lagoon.

Why would Onika seem suited to her tasks in such a boutique? Well, this freeway we're on isn't holding back anything that history gave birth to! After I remind myself of this, and feel justified, I continue: Driving, writing, reading. What's the difference now anyway?

The engineer couldn't help noticing what the girl he came to know as Onika was eating with a white plastic fork out of a Styrofoam box that must have been heated up in a microwave before she arrived. Rice, for sure, but soaked in a very dark gravy, almost black, and similar to the chunks of soft meat which broke easily under the prongs of her fork like strips of rotting rust-colored wood, the same color as her hair, hard to describe: like teased short coconut husk, dry, without hair-dressing, left to the wind's caprice. On his part, meaning, more than the war-lance history (whose history? Answer that yourself.) had plunged in the earth between them, there was hope for dialogue with their bodies: The eternal redeemer of everything that had already historically transpired between them; between every human: That is: their un-erasable human beginning.

"Excuse me, I hope I don't sound rude, but what's that you're eating?"

"Oh, this is 'Pepperpot' and rice."

"Did you get it at a Take-out around here? I've never seen or heard of it."

"No, I don't think you can get it around here, maybe out in one of those communities where immigrants from my homeland tend to live."

From head to toe (he noticed her nails were well kept but unpolished, and liked that) she was like black silk in her close-fitting white cotton skirt, soft khaki-colored linen shirt-jacket, pinched at the waist, with large thigh pockets, where once her cell phone buzzed and she read a brief text, sighing.

Her homeland, she mentioned, was in South America, but spoke English. He knew which country she meant, and saw data suddenly scrolling down a computer screen: Minerals, Agriculture, Floods, Socialism, Capitalism, Religious zeal, Ethnic insularity, IMF loans, Gold, Diamonds, Petroleum, Drug trafficking, US Visa scams, Deportees, the mass suicide of hundreds of American cultists in the jungle, books by all sorts of travelers and citizens who had left only with negative data and shallow impressions... but what about hospitality and hot sensual women? Never any of that! I felt a bit depressed and had to pull over quickly to the side of the freeway. There I saw a lot of wild bush with birds and ripe berries. That was comforting. I had more miles to complete on my way to the metropolis.

I drove off after day-dreaming. I noticed my hands on the steering wheel were white, and the remains of an old tomahauk lay in soft crinkled white crepe paper in a shoebox on the vacant seat beside me.

She was saying her homeland meal belonged to tribal native Indian cuisine: a complicated chemical extraction and spiced blend that the nomadic tribes who moved from place to place in cyclical cultivation and harvest had created to stand the test of time; never souring, never rotting and decaying, reheated, growing tastier with time and age; the same stew being added to for at least half a year with meats that were cured and flavored in its sauce.

He couldn't separate her from the sauce and vice versa on his stroll back to work, or later that night. The next day at lunch break he felt nervous on his walk back to the same spot, like a robot already programmed to repeat. He walked right by her sitting further up the promenade, where there was more space to sit. "Hey," she said, as though she knew he was looking for

her, and he sat down almost apologetically. He had lost the
necessity for an opening line because now she wasn't eating
Pepperpot, but Pastrami with tomatoes, salad, and Mayo on an
onion bun, along with her Starbucks coffee. "Gotcha!" she said
when she saw him at loss for words while staring at her bun.
Somehow his lunch was mostly always the same. The next day
she brought Chowmein with shredded chicken. That wasn't so
strange to him, who came looking and found her in another spot
not far from the one of the previous day. He asked her to lunch
for the next day, and she agreed. They went to a small Oriental
restaurant he knew, a few corners from the promenade. You
served yourself from a row of amazing dishes laid out along a
wall. On the weekend Friday, instead of going to the subway on
5th Avenue, and the number 3 train that took her to an affordable
one bedroom apartment far away in Brooklyn, she accepted his
offer for a drink.

She must have liked going with the flow, like how I was in
this freeway traffic, because even though I was tempted to tell her
of his African coffee-table books, the photographic Amazonian
tribal and ecological studies lining his bookcase and stacked
under the low coffee table resting on a large colorful Persian rug,
I resisted the urge. Let her find out for herself. She was an adult,
a big girl, nearly 30, I let him find that out too. There was no
fear or apprehension in her behavior, but whether that could be
attributed to the half dozen rock glasses of Mandarin Absolute
Vodka and Cranberry juice they had each consumed, no one will
ever know.

He kept the luscious abstract canvas with blobs of acrylic
color rushing vertically like pollen on a jungle river's muddy
surface, as a surprise for her to discover. And she revealed to his
delight that she knew of the elderly painter who lurched around
the metropolis like a drunken Bacchus, and was also originally

from her homeland. She sank down in a soft white armchair and contemplated the Australian aboriginal painting on white bark; the Robert Rauschenberg prints with New York neighborhoods and birds in cages; and a dazzlingly colorful Frank Stella wooden wall sculpture resembling Oceanic assemblages. She declined his offer to select a CD from his vast collection, and it was probably his choice of Anita O'Day backed by Gene Krupa and trumpeter Roy Eldridge on "Let Me off Uptown," which finally swept them into each other's arms.

There they are up there now, the lights of other tall old downtown apartments in Soho around his glowing through open Venetian blinds, as she brings to the dining table two soup bowls of very warm Pepperpot, left to 'sleep' for four days after being made from thick black 'casareep' stock imported and sold somewhere she knew of, then heated up. She is wearing nothing but a jingling gold bracelet with colorful little transparent plastic hearts, fake pearls and diamonds dangling from it. She looks like a shining night personified. While in the kitchen he, dressed in nothing more than briefs made from tanned animal skin printed fabric, chops up bananas, apples, peaches and grapes for a fruit salad with his Tarzan knife. She has taught him that stale old Pepperpot tastes better than fresh recently made one, especially with warm buttered toast. And as they break and dip pieces of toast into their bowls of the hot sticky stew, they glance at the TV from time to time, hearing CNN accounts of the latest Stock Market tremors, the financial crisis in Europe, the stalled government Health Care Bill, the over-heating earth, the recent suicide of a celebrity singer, and various racial crimes and attacks.

Meanwhile, on the freeway, I'm still racing towards their apartment in the metropolis for dinner. Even though I'm there already.

THE ICE-CREAM CHURN

S tuck in a cloud, unable to be touched, is the rusting shape of an ice-cream churn. Its rough skin of crusty tarnished metal canting into its crumbling wooden bucket.

It was between midnight and 1 am. The clock radio was still on, very low at Mozart's "Jupiter," the 4th Movement, he guessed. The distant siren of a patrol car went dipping in and out of the night along a nearby boulevard.

Then he was walking through an endlessly curving hallway between gift shops and cafes, out to the end of an airport terminal where people were bundled up in winter coats and hats, all seemingly of the same style or brand, the same as their clumsy running shoes. Their voices defined his difference from what did not include him it seemed, despite their similarity of origin and destination.

The rotting ice-cream churn remained somewhere on the horizon.

Next came his first day in a city of contemporary ruins, which made him laugh nervously as he sat in a hotel lobby with a view through its front door to the avenue and sidewalk. The same sidewalk where as a child he had been told to stick close to his mother and sisters among the throng of Christmas Eve shoppers flowing in and out of packed department stores, not one of which he could locate now. He saw himself walking down the avenue for lunch, crossing the street to a Chinese restaurant at a corner where an old Travel Agency building had stood, There, an American Soul singer in his sky blue linen suit, hair pressed shiny and slicked back, just as when he had first seen him on the front page of a morning newspaper with his band members smiling beside the propellers of a plane that had just brought them to the airport, was now sitting on his grey suitcase outside the unopened Travel Agency. He walked over to him and asked: "Are you Jackie Wilson?" already knowing he was, because of the front page photo and caption. The singer said: "Sure thing little man!"

That huge space of rubble across the street, visible from where he sat on a balcony before a plate of Prawns fried rice, would have been the school and church that each day he left at 3 pm to idle in the avenue (which led to him meeting the Soul singer), until picked up by his brother.

And where exactly was that ice-cream churn in all this?

He had a week to find out, so he walked up the avenue into his teenage youth of long and bushy-haired peers clutching just bought Faber and Penguin and Fontana paperbacks of their favorite writings by Lawrence Durrell, Edgar Mittelholzer, William Faulkner, Carson McCullers, Alberto Moravia, and others. He hurried to the concrete edge of flower beds outside a huge department store where they had sat with beautiful creole girls of dizzying skin color, hair textures, and vocal tones, but found instead concrete walls painted with fading sullied exotic landscapes (for tourists perhaps?) beside the cracked and stained sidewalk where drug addicts, vagrants, and stray dogs sprawled on blackened strips of cardboard. This was exactly where they often locked their bicycles to the store's iron railings before strolling around the spotless area meeting friends in light Mediterranean fashions influenced by the French and Italian movies they attended in groups. 'They' had vanished into big cities like the one he had just left.

The elusive, silent ruined antique ice-cream churn remained in his vision. One day, he realized it could have arisen from the sea-side village of his childhood.

So now he's walking down dusty noisy streets of this village baking in early afternoon sun. He's going by the faces of some old women under crumbling straw hats. They stare at him and smile with trembling lips, remembering the boy who had churned the ice cream they had savored on Christmas mornings at a school, when they were poor unwed teenage mothers. He paused to stare at that school, in a little street at whose corner up ahead an old soap factory, like an unpainted barn, had once fragranced the neighborhood's air. A street where at Christmas the young single mothers with their small children had been feted with ice-cream and fruit cake and gifts, like the other fortunate private house-holds in the neighborhood. The unwed single women and their children had been gifted by a league of securely married village women. One had been his mother, along with her sophisticated lively friend, who, when she visited, he had sat close to and thrilled at the tone of her attractive undulating voice and her orange gums in her smooth black enthusiastic face. A face and voice that since then always reminded him, for some unfathomable reason, of the ice-cream he had churned.

Reminded him now of the newly manufactured smell of orange, red, and blue sponge balls; the brightly painted glossy tin of finely manufactured little toy cars and trucks; of plastic whistles, silver Jacks, chubby dolls, rubber baby nursing bottles, powdered balloons, bubblegum on colored photo cards of cowboy movie stars, Tubby & Lulu, Mickey Mouse, and Donald Duck comic books, with their brand new glossy Dell covers and colored pages giving off the scent of fresh ink. Gifts for less secure children, all bought by the cash donations of various store owners in the village and downtown, wrapped in Christmas paper and tagged with those little cardboard strips illustrated with colorful bells, a Christmas tree, or Santa's smiling ruby face, then addressed to each recipient whose name his mother and her village friends had learnt. These unwrapped gifts he was warned not to touch, were kept at his home in wicker baskets.

The beaten eggs and poured evaporated milk sprinkled with essence of vanilla and grated nutmeg, were boiled to custard, then left to cool—its warm cream scooped off and eaten with his mother's permission—before filling the inner steel cistern of the ice-cream churn surrounded by hard broken ice sprinkled with salt and sawdust, he had operated, and now saw canting in a cloud, which slowly faded to cans of Carnation milk he was staring at in a New York supermarket, before he woke up.

INVISIBLE WRITING

Blackberries to their ears, Bally shoes on their feet stepping out of limousines onto congested avenues. Cautious unusual voices discussing invisible shores related to many difficult-to-pronounce first and last names, and the voiceless thanks on the faces of persons in khakis and Nikes, cheap jeans, garish shirts and blouses, off to push papers through cages for scrutiny, and rubber stamps eventually granting permission to throw out the garbage at Macdonalds, or mop the floor at Starbucks…or…

The writer couldn't find what next to write….

Ok. Here's something: 'Meanwhile, petroleum is bubbling thousands of feet beneath the ocean off a coastal shelf.' That's information inspired by foreign reports on the Internet; like other reports of gold bullion in the land's belly revolting against the indifference of Utopians to metallic wealth, which Raphael Nonsenso, a Portuguese sailor, had spoken of four centuries ago in More's 'UTOPIA'.

Reclining in his air-conditioned vehicle the new ambassador is being chauffeured to another press conference declaring the end of poverty, and the beginning of the ex-colony's and his country's new mutual wish for profit; the arrival of what was lacking in the form of a million years of rotting slimy compost become fuel in the thanks of hard-to-pronounce names happy to read in weekly immigrant tabloids about fortunes left intact for them back there…Somewhere that now, like More's 'UTOPIA',

146

feels like nowhere.

These written words are part of a text that's lying on the desk of a magazine editor. Only he sees them. If he publishes these words will he be seen as an accomplice to such frankness? What does this writer want anyway? Is the reader's pleasure sufficient? From up here it is a good thousand feet down to the crowded sidewalk of Blackberries, Bally shoes, sipped jumbo cardboard coffee cups, hot dog vendors, security guards, cognito and incognito. Does this information lie in the text on the editor's desk?

The writer with time to spare before his interview with the editor sat on the side of a large marble fountain and smoked a 'Capital' of the finest Virginia blend. He suddenly remembers tobacco was one of the first products from 'back there'.

He will write that sentence down in his next…what? Story? Essay? And? Will it satisfy his happiness?

The writer wishes his 'Capital' will never be consumed, because it has paused an anxious situation he will have to face again, meaning: writing this! His 'Capital' ends, and to avoid smoking another he walks off among the pretty girls in their short black dresses, their white shorts, their good legs leading him to wonder if what they secrete is different from all the experiences he has previously had with what are no longer secret legs.

The editor's office to the popular social magazine is up there somewhere. Inside the revolving doors. From the marble floor of the lobby the writer sees the name, the floor, the office number he needs on the wall behind the security man's desk. He does not have to wait long before the secretary acknowledges his name, wrapping up an agreement with an advertiser, before wiring her voice through to the editor's desk behind her wall.

It's serious fun guessing this young (handsome, like Rock Hudson, but blond-haired, not parted, just brushed back) editor's thoughts about the writer. Who will be the first to dismiss the

difference in race between them? How will anyone know who
is the first? Will the outcome of this interview be unaffected by
history, knowledge, ignorance, fantasy, desire, expectations?

"These people, on this page," the editor says to the writer,
"with their strong creole accent..." He would have liked to hear
more about these people (who seemed to him more the 'real
people' of wherever they're from), a whole series of articles
on such people he suggests, somehow suddenly thinking of the
Vicynoisse soup, Beef Wellington sandwich on rye, escargot,
Black Forest cake, and latte he will have in half-an-hour in an
exclusive restaurant a block away, where the accents eating will
be like his, or like the European Union, or...well, not like these
people on this page before him that he wants to hear more about,
or...well...maybe except for a busboy or two.

That's an expensive striped Ralph Lauren shirt the writer is
wearing beneath his double-breasted black jacket. He cuts an
elegant figure. Those are olive-green suede Hush Puppies on
his feet. The editor notices these facts, recalling a vague rumor
among his professional peers that the writer is a womanizer, a
Ladies man, like Ernie Kovacs in Strangers When We Meet, as
they shake hands to no agreement, as yet.

The writer walks out and begins scribbling this (as he waits
on an elevator), on the blank side of his manuscript the public
has not read as yet.

If you loved this book, would you please provide a review at Amazon.com?

Lightning Source UK Ltd.
Milton Keynes UK
UKOW04n1427021117
312071UK00002B/19/P